KATHMANDU

LUKE RICHARDSON

PROLOGUE

The building shook with the explosion. Heat, dust and debris billowed in every direction. Metal crunched against concrete. The lights flickered and then died.

All was quiet.

Somewhere on the street, a car alarm yelped twice before silencing itself. A pair of ceiling tiles fell from their mountings and crashed to the floor. Escaping water hissed from somewhere nearby.

The two men sheltering behind the thick concrete wall heard very little. Heavy-duty ear defenders made sure of that. They would have felt it, though. The force would have rattled through their bones, as they sat, bodies tensed against the wall.

The men looked around the dark room.

The larger of the two snapped on a torch and swept it over the destruction. A light fixing swayed on its wire. A desk lay on its side, papers and files scattered across the carpet. Broken glass peppered the floor around an empty window. A notice board lay on its side, its contents shredded by the blast.

The second man stood and whistled as he took in the devastation. "That did the job," he said, facing his colleague.

The larger man nodded and turned towards the explosion's epicentre. The finger of light from his torch swept through the dust hanging thick in the air. The other man followed.

The closer they got, the denser the dust became.

"Time lock my arse," the first one said, his voice muffled by the face mask. "I knew we'd get it open." It sounded as though he was smiling.

Both men wore masks just in case any cameras had survived the blast. The masks also helped with the dust. These guys knew what they were doing. Ultimate professionals.

Powdered concrete danced in the beams as they swept across the room before converging on a pile of twisted metal on the floor.

"Piece of cake," the other man said, his torch rising to illuminate the gnarled gap where the vault's door had stood steadfast just moments ago.

"It's lucky no one knows this place is here, though."

On an industrial park in Brighton's suburbs, there were few residents to consider at this time of day. The men had already taken care of the two-person security detail. They would wake up in a few hours after some very lucid dreams.

"We better get moving, car alarms will be going off from here to Lewis." The first man stepped over the twisted door and into the vault.

Rows of safety deposit boxes in various sizes made up three walls of the small room. Each had a number and a keyhole.

"Look at this place," said the second man. "Imagine all the —"

"We're just here for one box," the other man cut in. He turned the torch on his colleague. "Don't even think about that. We get what we came for, then we get out of here. We're getting paid enough for this already. Understand?"

"Yeah, course."

"Box 288, there, look." He pointed across the room with his gloved hand. "Get that open. Then we're gone."

1

Sundown in Kathmandu.

A blinding orange sun sinks through a fragmented wall of clouds. Shafts of haggard, uncompromising light signal the falling blanket of dusk. Behind the sprawling city, the silver backs of the Himalayas stand resolute.

The clang and yammer of daytime production mutes as merchants, makers and menders pack away the tools of their trade. A welder, a bicycle repairman, a tyre salesman. Their work for the day complete and their concern for the hunger of their families met. In the upstairs windows, lights begin to blaze. The smell of spice and onions replaces the oil, paint and rubber.

Two young men make their way through a backstreet. Kathmandu is a warren of them, allowing people to scuttle unseen. Concrete structures stand tall on both sides, leaving a narrow, dusty path. The going is difficult. They know it'll be worth it.

As they turn left at a crossroads, the narrow passage forces them into single file. They walk in silence. The man in front lights a cigarette; it flares in the shadows. The sky is just a strip of dirty orange between the buildings. It's a constant glowing reminder of human creation.

The residents are used to these people. A rabble of them have passed through their city, homes and restaurants for as long as anyone can remember. For some, it's the beginning of a journey — perhaps Pokhara, or Everest. For others, it's the end. A final stop before the road becomes impassable, inconvenient or uncomfortable, and the flight home beckons.

The men walk towards the end of the passage, a dead end — the concrete wall of a building. Its ugly construction is bulky and mysterious in the darkness. Pipes and wires bulge like veins across its skin.

They know what they seek. They need to look for the light.

A bare bulb, swinging on its wire and encircled by insects, hangs above a door. It's the only thing that separates the door the men are seeking from any other.

Soon darkness will embody the sky, though not the city. Residents keep their lights burning, believing that with darkness comes trouble. Trouble they could no better see than understand. Trouble they should have forgotten long ago.

The door opens before the men reach it. A man with an oily smile stands in the gloom. Nodding as they enter, the man shows them to a table in the dark room. The small restaurant is kept dark on purpose.

"You want the lamb, we have the lamb again," he says when they're seated. The men nod, order beers and resume their conversation.

They're travelling on tomorrow, out into the mountains,

hiking somewhere. The waiter can't work out where even in the quiet of the empty restaurant.

The waiter places bottled beers on the table; neither of the young men look up. Then he hangs back in the shadows, listening.

"Looking forward to leaving this city…" one says to the other.

"Yeah, it's not been…"

From the scraps of conversations, the waiter makes a decision.

"There are so many other places…"

"We're getting out tomorrow…"

The oily grin runs across his face as he clicks a switch on the wall. The light outside — *look for the light* — dies into darkness.

2

I'm going to kiss you now, Leo thinks, his confidence burgeoning from an evening of shared drinks, smiles and laughs.

I'm going to kiss you now. It's the second time he and Mya have met. It's going well.

They started drinking in a wood-beamed pub in the Lanes hours ago. The night was busy. People stumbled in groups from one place to the next, but Leo hadn't noticed any of them. A basement cocktail bar. Metal stairs, gleaming bar stools, low lighting. A booth at the back designed for those taking part in a night for two.

And then they were out, laughing in the lustrous morning air. 4 am.

"Where to now?" Mya asks, crossing her arms against the chill.

"India!" Leo shouts.

Mya giggles and puts her arm through his. "Go on then," she says. "Take me to India."

I'm going to kiss you now, Leo thinks again as he gazes at the curving domes of the Royal Pavilion float in the milky pinks of summertime pre-dawn. The garden's tall flowers mirror the sky with dew-covered leaves.

I'm going to kiss you now, Leo thinks as they drink from cans on a bench in the glinting air. Mya wears his jacket and curves her shape into his. Leo tries not to notice the cold as his hand slips down her back. He traces the contours of her figure beneath the dress he's been looking at all night. They've built a bubble around them which is theirs alone. The world is now just the two of them. This is his moment — their moment.

The sun warns of its impending arrival as purple shoots across the clear sky, colouring every surface of the ivory pavilion. Time is short. Once the sun comes, their bubble will fade with the waking city.

Leo takes a sip of his beer. *Breathe. Do it.*

"I'm going to kiss you now," he says, hearing the words before his drunken ears knew they'd been spoken.

Mya looks up at him, her eyes absorbing the colour from the sky.

The kiss is hot, sexy, steamy and longing. It's all he's wanted and more. Her skin is soft beneath his.

They kiss until they're kissing more than not. They're in their own world — a planet just for them. Leo inhales the smell of her neck as passion passes boiling point. He wants to live in this moment forever. He doesn't want it to end, but he knows it will with the rising sun.

Neither notice as the light fades from aubergine to peach.

"Oi, get out of here!" comes a voice from the direction of the pavilion. "What're you doing? You shouldn't be here!"

A security guard jogs towards them.

Leo pulls on Mya's hand — time to go. One more kiss as she stands.

The bubble's burst — the world's alive. Buses pull sleepy passengers to work, people walk dogs, and the large security man runs after them.

Over the fence, they giggle back into the city.

Mya rummages through her bag for the key, fits it into the lock and leads Leo in. The bed's still covered with the dresses she'd laid there earlier.

From where Leo lies, the light catches Mya's jawline, her strong cheekbones, her figure. Her dress slips to the floor in a mix of excitement and awe. Her body's a silhouette. Mya moves towards him, but he's already there, already living it. They roll like thunder into the darkness, into the silence.

3

———————

Leo woke, lifted his head and looked around. He wasn't in bed. In front of his unfocused eyes, the two screens of his computer glowed in the darkness and beyond them rain hammered against the greasy glass of the window. He rubbed his face and stretched. *What time is it?*

He glanced at the clock on the screen. 5 am. The sun would soon be making an appearance.

A number of notifications on the screen demanded Leo's attention. He squinted at them and the symbols danced in front of his eyes.

How long have I been asleep?

Since losing his job a week ago, Leo had spent almost every waking hour at his computer. He felt as though he were losing track of time in general. He gazed past the fingers of rain lashing the window and towards the darkened sea. All he thought about was Mya.

He had been looking for her for nearly two years. Every night he sat at his computer and scrolled though possible leads; now he didn't have a job he could do it in the daytime too. He sorted through pictures, social media posts, articles and videos. Separated those that could be her from those that definitely weren't. Leo analysed anything that could provide him with an explanation about where Mya had gone.

The way Leo saw it, she was either dead or had chosen to go. Neither option was good. Neither brought him solace. But he needed something.

Leo reached for the cup of coffee on the table beside him, lifted it to his lips and grimaced at the taste of the cold liquid.

When Mya first disappeared, friends and family had been supportive, meeting his morose moods with concerned smiles and empathy.

Anything you need, let us know.

That soon changed into offers to help him move on, find someone new.

You can't spend your whole life looking for her.

Then, as Leo declined invitations in favour of the search, friends became just irksome distractions. Figures hanging unseen on his life's periphery.

Leo struggled out of his seat and stretched. At least now, without work to worry about, he had more time to spend on the search. If there was ever a perfect opportunity to find her, this was it.

4

In the restaurant, the men eat wordlessly. The lamb is as spectacular as ever. Perfectly spiced, sizzling, succulent and fresh. They abandon cutlery and eat with their hands, grabbing at the meat by its bones, skin and muscle.

Although meat is served in Kathmandu, it's not the norm. The pair have been in the city a few days, and they've seen nothing like the lamb served at the backstreet restaurant.

"They get it from the mountains," they'd been told by a guy they'd met on their first afternoon in the city. "It's the best meat in Kathmandu, if you can find the place. The lambs live up in the mountains where they eat wild grasses and breathe the fresh air. That's what makes them so big and strong. Most restaurants here don't serve it — or save it for their best customers. This place, if you can find it, is amazing."

Later that evening, they'd followed the guy's directions down the passageways, each one smaller than the last. By some luck they found their way to the dark door advertised only by the bare bulb.

They'd been back three times since. Each time greeted by the waiter with the oily smile. Each time ordering the succulent, delicious, Himalayan Lamb.

From the kitchen door, the waiter stands and watches them. The waiter's smile is unchanged, unflinching. Ever oily.

One man tears meat from a long bone with his teeth. The other picks at it, the way a vulture devours an abandoned carcass.

When the two men finish eating the waiter approaches to collect the dishes. The men stretch backwards to rest their full stomachs. Sweat mottles their pink foreheads.

"You want our special smoke?" the waiter asks. The diners' fingers are tinted red from the spices. They look at each other.

"We do have an early bus to catch," one replies.

"It's free because you are special customers, coming back again. It's a family tradition."

They exchange smiles. They're in Kathmandu. How can they refuse?

The waiter stands a large, ornate shisha pipe on the floor next to them and lights the coals on top. Four hoses curl from the white body upon which engraved snakes dance. Their scales shimmer in the dark restaurant. The waiter draws hard on one of the hoses. Liquid gurgles and the red eyes of coal glow ferociously. He pulls again until the smoke comes through thick and white.

"With our compliments," he says, passing the hose to one of the men. Then, bowing slightly he returns to the shadows. His oily smile remains.

"Kathmandu isn't all that bad," one man says to the other, picking up the pipe and taking a drag.

"Don't have too much, we're on the nine am bus tomorrow."

It will not make a difference, the waiter thinks from the shadows.

5

S team curled from the kettle as it rattled to the boil and clicked off. Leo dumped a tablespoon of instant coffee in a cup, added a splash of milk, and filled it with the boiling water.

The sky was beginning to lighten outside, although the grizzly rain still pounded against the glass. Winter was coming, and the flat was getting cold. Leo rubbed his hands together then did up the zipper on his hoody. He glanced at the boiler. He should put the heating on, but since he'd lost his job paying the bills had become problematic.

It had all been some stupid misunderstanding. Another journalist recorded part of a court case and broadcast the video on the newspaper's social media channels. Social media channels that were Leo's responsibility.

Leo padded through to the front room, the biggest in his third floor flat. He lived in one of the large Victorian terrace houses that line Brighton's streets. Once grand, the house had many years ago been split into four. Leo's small portion of it was right at the top. He'd lived in the flat for so long that he now found the curling wallpaper, threadbare carpets and drafty windows homely. His desk was nestled in the bay window. On a good day he could see the sea sparkling to the left. Today though the air hung thick and grey as the rain hammered the greasy glass.

I really should get those curtains fixed, Leo mused, *then I wouldn't have to look out at the pounding weather.*

Slumping down at his desk, Leo shook the mouse and the computer twitched to life. On one screen the website he ran appeared: Missing People International. On the other, a program continuously searched the Internet. The search was based around the most recent images he had of Mya. It included the locations she wanted to visit, carefully chosen keywords and a more general description. It had been running non-stop almost two years.

A dialogue box flashed in the centre of the screen. It displayed an article from a Peruvian newspaper. Clicking the box, a page of Spanish text appeared before being translated automatically by the software. The article was about two so far unnamed British tourists who'd died in a climbing accident. Scanning through, Leo found that neither was twenty-eight, the age Mya would now be. He moved it to the 'Read' folder so the system wouldn't bring it up again.

Leo took a sip of the coffee. The room was a reminder of his mission. The mission his life had become. The articles Leo was unable to dismiss surrounded a map of the world on the wall. He pinned them up, hoping to see a pattern. One day, two might match and lead to something — a clue to where Mya had gone.

A notification appeared from the Missing People International forum. It was the most popular part of the site, a vibrant community of people with one, sad, common factor — someone they loved was lost. To read it was heart-breaking. Leo had to remind himself of the importance of his work. It wasn't only about him getting closer to finding Mya. It was also helping the hundreds or thousands of people with unanswered questions in their lives. A question mark hanging where once existed a man, woman or child.

The notification was a post from a lady in Cyprus looking for her son who'd not been seen in two weeks. Leo knew the feeling. He dealt with it every day. Posting the link for the "Things to do when a loved one is missing" page on the website, and a personal note, he closed the email window. Another person with a part of their life gone. He wished her well. In reality, Leo knew there was very little anyone could do.

Two years ago, when Mya had disappeared, Leo didn't know anything about missing people. He had so many questions. What to do first? What authorities to contact? How do you make the local police take it seriously? Leo assumed there were people whose job it was to find those who were missing. It was a painful realisation when he learned there weren't. Police forces around the world are stretched thin. When an adult goes missing, it's assumed they want to be lost, and will, maybe one day, just come back.

Leo sat back in the chair and listened to the rain thrashing against the glass. Mya was out there somewhere.

Leo was determined to find out where.

6

Sometimes in life you just have to run.

Fuli had passed the door many times whilst she'd been kept in the house. She'd noticed the outside world glinting mysteriously through the glass, but had never thought to try the handle. Until today.

She knew he was expecting her in the back room. He'd shouted for her to come down only moments ago. He'd be expecting her to come through the curtain soon.

He'd be having a hushed conversation with the man who had just arrived. They'd be acting like old friends, talking about her, and exchanging piles of dirty money. All of that would stop, replaced by false smiles as she entered.

Fuli knew what would happen behind the curtain. She'd been there often enough.

She had despised it in the beginning. The cold, callused touch of the sort of men that arrived made her skin crawl. But then she grew used to it — the idle chatter, the commands, her compliance. A few minutes after, time would be hers again. Some took longer than others, but none took that long.

Today could be different, she thought, holding the door open. The fresh breeze of the Kathmandu afternoon streamed in. She had felt the breeze many times before from behind the bars of her third floor window. It was never this intoxicatingly close.

"Fuli, get in here!" came his voice, rough and rank from smoking and whiskey. She knew the smell. He kept her for himself sometimes when he'd had too much. "Don't keep your visitor waiting." It sounded as if he were smiling. He was probably sharing a joke, counting the visitor's money and telling him dirty things about her.

Fuli teetered with the possibility. She could close the door again. No one would ever know she'd even thought about it. Or she could try her luck out there.

It isn't bad here, she thought, high on opportunity but scared of unfamiliarity. She was one of the lucky ones, he'd said, one of his favourites. Others forced their girls to do all sorts of things. He had rules, though. He respected her, and made sure her visitors did too.

Fuli remembered what it was like when she'd first been brought here. She thought about his hot and sour breath against her face for the first time. That was months ago now, even years. Fuli remembered it though — as clear as the traffic through the gap in the door. She remembered sitting on the stained mattress in the room upstairs after he had finished with her. Feeling the place where he had been. He liked to be the first. That's what he'd said.

"You little bitch, get down here now." His voice was aggressive now. He'd moved closer to the curtain which obscured the back room from the door.

Fuli peered through the gap. The invigorating possibility. The traffic noise swirled around her. The smell of fumes was noxious and exciting. A brightly-coloured bus pulled near. Enthusiastic people gazed through the smeared windows. All of them going somewhere. People visiting their families, or tourists going hiking in the mountains. Wherever they were going, they were excited and happy. Free. They were not confined to a dirty mattress in a dark room, waiting for his call.

As the bus pulled closer, Fuli noticed a group of Nepali men through the front window. They spoke excitedly, with animated expressions. Maybe it was their first journey together — *a journey she deserved too.*

Fuli stepped through the door, towards grumbling traffic and the potent smell of the city. She felt the bright daylight warm her skin. She glanced nervously over her shoulder and pulled the door closed behind her.

7

Skillful hands separate skin from flesh, flesh from bone. The men have a lot to prepare before the restaurant opens tonight. They work quietly in the kitchen. Each man cutting, splitting, pulling, before seasoning with the spices decided by generations past.

In two hours, the sun will struggle beneath the mountains surrounding the city and the bulb above the door will burn. Neither of the men question how their restaurant is found each night, but they know it will be. Those wanting adventure, wanting to experience something new and secret, will seek it out. They need to be ready. The Himalayan Lamb needs to be ready.

8

Leo flopped down at his computer and sorted through what the search bots had thrown up overnight. There was a picture taken at a concert with a number of blurred faces. The computer system had highlighted one of them. Leo squinted at the screen then thumbed the delete button — that wasn't her. The smile just wasn't right. Leo would recognize Mya's smile anywhere.

The problem was, none of these sightings seemed to be getting him anywhere. It was nearly two years since Mya had gone missing and Leo had no clue about where she was.

Leo knew that Mya loved to travel, so part of him thought he should be out there looking for her. He just didn't know where to start. Plus, the outside world brought with it the unknown, and the unknown made Leo anxious.

He scrolled to the next image which the computer system thought could be Mya. He rejected that one too.

Leo then turned to his email and scrolled through the junk mail he'd received overnight. He deleted a dozen about web-hosting and relationships with cheeky looking Russian women. Then he paused over one from an address he didn't recognize. His finger hovered over the delete button. Something stopped him. An echo of familiarity over the name. Blake Stockwell.

SUBJECT: Assistance needed to find my missing daughter.

Dear Mr Keane,

It is with regret that I write to you as I fear I have few options left. My youngest daughter, Allissa, has been out of communication with the family for nearly two years. She is now twenty-eight years old. We have recently come into some new information, which, although possibly mistaken, may indicate her whereabouts. My wife and I are unable to go ourselves. Obviously, we could send someone else, but we would like to do this discreetly, hence my contacting you. I understand you reside in Brighton. We will be visiting this weekend. We will be staying at the Grand Hotel. Please call the hotel to arrange a meeting. I will give you a full precis of the facts as we understand them in person.

Yours sincerely, and with thanks.

Lord B. Stockwell

9

Fuli squinted against the bright afternoon sun as she took her first steps of freedom. The street around her thronged with bikes, taxis and cars. It felt a million miles from the small village in which she grew up.

"What are you doing? Get back here!"

He must have heard the door shut behind her. His voice sounded different outside — distant, yet still angry and worse, dangerous. She didn't want to go back. She couldn't go back. She ran.

She turned left and then right without daring to look behind her. She didn't want to see his outstretched arms, ready to take her back to that house, that room, those men.

Fuli ran towards a crowd of people ahead. Her feet ached. Her thin shoes were no match for the turbulent road. She overtook slowing cars and dived into a crowded market. She pushed past people, only hearing their protests as she passed. One more reason not to stop. She couldn't stop now.

She had to keep going.

10

"Namaste. How are you?" Allissa said, practicing the Nepalese she'd been learning. Her mouth stumbled over the unfamiliar words.

The market seller sitting cross-legged behind a pyramid of tomatoes smiled in surprise.

"I'm fine but hot," he replied, his eyes turning towards the bright afternoon sky.

Allissa beamed — she'd been understood, although his answer was lost on her.

The market bustled around her. Within this small area, the sprawling concrete of the city was replaced by strips of coloured cloth stacked with spices, vegetables, fruit and flowers.

Watching the other browsers, Allissa knelt, picked one of the tomatoes from the pile, then brought it close to her face and inhaled the sweet fragrance. It had taken most of her life and half the world to know how to take her time.

In England, where she'd grown up, people always wanted to be somewhere else and never actually enjoyed where they were. In the last year, she'd realised how that attitude strained the simple pleasures from life. The texture of tomatoes ripening in the sun. The smell of the spices at the next stall, spoonfuls of which the seller would deposit onto a large hollowed rock and crush and mix to the buyer's specification.

Time was ultimately all anyone had; it was what you did with it that mattered.

The distant sound of traffic grumbled behind the chatter of negotiation.

"Just these," Allissa said, dropping six tomatoes into her bag. The seller tilted his head from side to side as he calculated his first price. Agreeing on a sale in Kathmandu could entail a negotiation of some minutes. It was one custom Allissa had come to enjoy during her time in Asia.

Two minutes later, she slid a collection of coins into the seller's outstretched hand and stepped into the stream of people. She still needed onions, spices and yoghurt for their meal.

Allissa paused at a stall of incense to breathe in the scent of sandalwood. The seller offered her the burning stick.

"Watch out!" came a shout from somewhere nearby, followed by a movement that caught Allissa's eye.

A rush of feet. A crescendo of voices. Then the world blurred, and something hard struck her elbow.

Allissa fell, sprawling to the concrete. Shouts of complaints and concern erupted as shoppers reached to steady and help. A pile of onions bounced and skittered across the floor. Allissa looked around in a daze. On the floor beside her a girl scrambled to her feet. The girl's dark eyes were tear-filled. Blood oozed from a long scratch on her leg.

"Are you okay?" Allissa asked, losing all concern for herself. "Are you hurt?"

The girl stared at Allissa without understanding. Allissa's lessons in Nepalese were coming up short, though she recognized the instinctive, pleading look of fear in the girl's expression.

"Mānisakō, Mānisakō." The girl pointed frantically in the direction she'd come: *the man, the man.*

Allissa stood and looked around. Across the market, next to the stuttering traffic, a large Nepalese man scanned the crowd. The way he moved told Allissa he wasn't there to shop.

"This way." Allissa pulled the girl by the arm. "Keep low."

Pushing people aside, they made it to the opposite side of the market where stalls again crawled with foot traffic.

Allissa turned to see the man, his muscles taut under a discolored white t-shirt as he looked left, then right. Then he headed their way.

11

Leo paused outside the ornate doors of the Grand Hotel and turned to face the sea. He looked out at the horizon, where the grey sky kissed the grey ocean. He shuddered as light rain peppered against his face.

Leo couldn't believe he was doing this. He wasn't some kind of detective. He was an out of work journalist who knew a bit about finding people, not someone who went around the world looking for them. He inhaled a deep gulp of the sea air to quell the anxiety creeping across his chest.

A pair of seagulls skipped through the sky above him, their mournful cries lost in the rumble of the wind. Glancing at them distractedly, thoughts of Mya began to swarm through Leo's mind. She had been the only thing that made his anxiety bearable. From the moment they'd met, his life had seemed more purposeful and complete. She gave him something to think about when the anxiety threatened. Something to focus on as he clawed through it. Someone who would listen without judgement. With her, there was a calm that now, and before they'd met, eluded him.

Over the years he'd tried many things to control it. He'd seen specialists. He'd been on drugs for a while. He'd even learned breathing exercises and coping strategies. Yet, Mya was the only real cure he had found.

Leo watched the seagulls pounding down the seafront.

And now Mya was gone. He took another deep breath, held it in his lungs for a moment, pulled open the door and stepped inside.

The Grand Hotel was as elaborate as Leo had expected it to be. Although he'd run past the building many times, glancing in at the soft lighting and sumptuous furniture, he'd never actually been inside.

"Can I help you sir?" asked the receptionist. Leo explained he had an arrangement to meet a guest in the hotel's bar.

"If you'd follow me," the man said, leading Leo across the soft carpet and through a door.

"There's a young man here to see you," the receptionist said as they approached a figure sitting alone at a dark table in the gloomy bar.

"Bring him over then," the waiting figure snapped in reply, before turning and seeing Leo. "Mr Keane." Stockwell stood and offered Leo his hand.

"Lord Stockwell," Leo said, struggling out of his coat.

"Blake, please," Stockwell replied. His hand was moist and flabby. "Would you like a drink? I can recommend the Glendronach." Stockwell lifted his glass and the ice cubes clinked.

"Yes, that would be good," Leo replied. "I'll have the same."

"This is a fine hotel," Stockwell said, returning to his seat. "I've had many memorable nights here. Been coming to

Brighton almost fifty years. There was one particularly memorable night. We were here for a conference in the eighties, eighty-four I think it was... Someone put a bomb underneath the Prime Minister's bath, totally ruined everyone's sleep." Stockwell took a deep sip of the whisky. "Anyway, I've not asked you here to share stories. This is a serious matter."

Leo's drink arrived. "Yes, of course. How can I help you, Lord Stockwell?"

"It concerns my daughter. My youngest, Allissa." Stockwell had a way of speaking that made the whole lower part of his face wobble. "She's always been a problem to us, never wanted to do any of the things the other girls did. We sent her to the best schools, and she did well but has never been interested in using her qualifications. She's got this idea in her head about trying to change the world. The more we spent on her education, the more she used it to rail against us." He paused for another sip. "I mean, I'm no monster, but I just don't see the appeal for a young, beautiful, intelligent girl to help a bunch of people who're doing nothing to help themselves."

"I understand." Leo wondered whether him helping Stockwell would be doing exactly that.

"Good. Well, it all came to a head two years ago. She'd graduated from Cambridge. Did very well. Written a thesis about some socialist nonsense, but it was good, apparently. Anyway, Eveline, my wife, secured her a contract at a local law firm. The perfect opportunity. Would've got her career off to a flying start. We knew she was reluctant, but thought it was just nerves, and that she'd be alright once she got started. Anyway, a couple of weeks before her graduation, she just disappeared. No goodbye. No nothing."

Stockwell lifted the drink to his lips again. His face reddened with each swallow.

"Eveline was distraught. I thought Allissa would be back in a couple of weeks. Allissa had always been argumentative, as I said, but she'd never actually left before. We got a call a few days later, when she told us she was going travelling for a bit. There was a savings account with a fair amount of money in it. Not that much, but I'm told it was enough to travel and live a basic lifestyle for some time."

"Do you know where she went?"

"South America or Asia, somewhere like that." Stockwell grimaced.

"Do you know where she is now?"

"Well, we've heard nothing for over a year. She's over eighteen, so we can't track her accounts. A couple of months ago she called, quite out of the blue, and asked her sister to transfer a large sum of money from a trust fund into a Nepalese account in Kathmandu. Thirty-five grand..."

Leo's eyes widened.

"Lucy, her sister, transferred the money before telling us. That was the deal Allissa had made with her. She said she didn't mind us knowing after the transfer had been made." Stockwell drained his glass. "Obviously, we were relieved to know she was safe." His voice became an angry crescendo. "But... I mean, what could she possibly be doing with thirty-five grand in Kathmandu?" Stockwell shook his glass in the air and the waiter collected it.

Leo shook his head. "How can I help you with this? Surely you can look online?"

"No, we've tried that. Nothing. The more we look, the more worried we become. Kathmandu seems to be full of all sorts of unsavoury people. No telling what they do out there. They're savages." Stockwell knitted his fingers together, leaned on the table and looked directly at Leo. "You are to go to Kathmandu and find her. Find our Allissa."

Leo's anxiety rose. Sure, he'd travelled before, but that was with Mya. She'd known what she was doing. She made it easy for him. His chest tightened and he concentrated on his breathing.

Breathe in.

Stockwell sat up and put his hands on the arms of the chair.

"Obviously, we'd pay for your time and costs. This is very important to us."

Breathe out.

Leo knew the money would be useful now he didn't have a job, but this wasn't his thing. He wasn't a detective. Leo focused harder on his breathing as the anxiety took hold.

Breathe in.

"Shall we say ten grand upfront and five more when you get to Kathmandu?"

Leo's chest tightened further at the thought. Sure, looking online, Leo could do that. But going to an unknown city on the other side of the world...

Leo stuttered an answer. His hand tensed around the glass. He needed to concentrate on his breathing.

Breathe out.

Panic rose, tight breathing suffocating his mind.

Breathe in.

The opulent surroundings of the bar suddenly felt claustrophobic to Leo. He sunk back into the chair. Retreating. Stockwell's unblinking gaze pinned him to the spot.

Breathe out.

Got to get out, he thought, making to get up. *Got to stop.*

Breathe in.

Focus.

Breathe out.

Behind Leo, two women walked through the doorway's rectangle of daylight. Both were glamorous, tall, striking silhouettes. Stockwell's eyes darted after them.

Leo felt a slight release without the Lord's stare pinning him down.

Breathe in. The oxygen soothed his lungs. *And breathe out.*

The women walked out into the sunlight. Stockwell's eyes returned to Leo. He took another deep breath and exhaled slowly. The tension began to shift.

"You know, Lord Stockwell... Blake. I'd love to help you. But I'm not a detective." Leo took a sip of the whisky. "I'm just someone who's lost someone too. I do try to help other people in any way I can." He paused. One quick inhale. One slow exhale. "But I've never gone and actually looked for them."

"I think you've misinterpreted me... Leo." Stockwell pronounced the name as though it might break. "I may not agree with all the decisions my daughter has made, but I am her father, and I am concerned for her safety. I cannot rest thinking she might be involved in something horrible over there, in Kathmandu." His face contorted at the word. "I... I mean we, my wife and I — our whole family — we just want her home, or at least to know she's safe."

Watching Stockwell struggle over the words, Leo felt an understanding. He knew what it was like to need answers. If it were Mya in Kathmandu, then Leo knew he'd go in an instant.

With the warm sensation of the whisky reaching his stomach, Leo thought about Mya's insatiable sense for adventure. A never-ending thirst for new and exciting experiences. Leo took another sip and felt the possibilities start a fire of willingness. A fire that quickly began to take hold.

He did need the money.

"If you'll do it..." Stockwell paused, watching Leo's conflict. "If you do it, that would be great. I really want you to. If you can't... well, I'll find someone else who will."

"Okay, I'll" — Leo heard the words before he knew he was saying them — "I'll do it."

Filtered by long net curtains, the late afternoon light poured through the window. Darkness was some hours off, but the shadows had started to elongate toward the evening.

Fuli sat at one end of the bed with her chin resting on her hands. Her face was streaked where the tears had fallen. Now her eyes were dry and empty.

"There you are, that's looking much better," Allissa said, kneeling on the floor to clean the scratch on Fuli's right shin. Fuli looked up, offering a weak smile.

"When Chimini gets home," Allissa said, ignoring the fact she knew the girl wouldn't understand, yet afraid to let the silence go too far, "she'll explain everything. We'll talk. It'll be good to get to know you. The most important thing is that you know you're safe here."

A metallic ding drew Allissa's attention to the door, through which the brightness of the guest house's reception area glowed.

"I'll be right back," Allissa said. "You're totally safe here."

A young man stood at the reception desk. He was tanned and held his rucksack easily across one shoulder.

"Hi, can I help you?" Allissa said, crossing the room.

"Yes, hi. I'm looking for a room tonight. I just got here, and saw your sign outside."

"We've got nothing available tonight, I'm sorry," Allissa said without checking the register. They still needed to buy furniture for the tourists' rooms. "I am sorry. Try downstairs."

"No problem. Will do," the man said, turning back towards the stairs. The guesthouse occupied just one floor of a building above two similar operations.

"Just someone looking to see if they could stay here," Allissa said out loud as she pushed the bedroom door open. "But we've not got any room. I need to —"

She looked into the bedroom and stopped. The girl had gone.

13

Leo sat opposite Lord Stockwell in the bar of the Grand Hotel and tried to work out if the unnatural exposure of his teeth was supposed to be a grin.

Stockwell slid a dark leather briefcase onto the table between them, then unlocked it and rummaged through the contents. He removed a yellow folder and passed it to Leo.

"In here is everything you'll need. Copies of recent photographs. A description of her. Details of her interests." He closed the briefcase and returned it to the floor.

Leo opened the folder and found four typed sheets of A4 paper and two photographs. He scanned the first sheet of notes and saw the details Stockwell had mentioned. He would have to read it in detail later. Leo turned over the page and saw the first of the pictures. To Leo's surprise, the image that stared back at him didn't look anything like Stockwell. Allissa was beautiful. She had a bright smile and radiant eyes. In contrast to the large man that sat in front of him, she had dark skin. Leo looked from the picture to Stockwell and back again. There were similarities, but Allissa obviously got her complexion from her mother.

"How many daughters have you got?" Leo asked, looking up at the Lord.

Stockwell sat up a little straighter at the question. "Two daughters and one son."

Leo asked a couple more questions, and each time Stockwell answered them simply.

"The more I know," Leo said, "the better understanding I'll have of Allissa. That'll help me find her."

Leo looked back at the picture and realized why Stockwell had chosen it. This was the mental image he had of his daughter. In the picture, a relaxed Allissa walked through a field, as though on a countryside stroll.

Leo turned over to the next picture.

"She sent this one to her sister about a year ago," Stockwell said, watching Leo myopically.

In this photograph, Allissa sat on a beach looking over her right shoulder at the camera. To Leo, it looked much more like the sort of picture Allissa would choose of herself. She looked healthy, happy and free. Behind her, a deserted beach rolled into palm groves. Her dark hair fell over her shoulders. Her skin was clear and glowing.

"It's the most recent photograph we have. I wasn't going to include it, but Eveline said I should."

"She looks happy in it," Leo told him. "It's a nice picture."

Stockwell grumbled and looked at his watch. "I'll leave that with you." Stockwell pulled a cheque book and pen from his jacket pocket. He filled in the cheque then held it out for Leo. "Ten thousand pounds. Send me your account details, and I'll wire you the rest when you get to Kathmandu."

Leo looked at the cheque in Stockwell's extended grasp.

The gold embossed letters of the bank's unusual logo glimmered.

"I want updates every two days," Stockwell said. "Don't think you can sit on your arse and still get paid." His grey eyes narrowed harshly as Leo reached for the cheque.

"I'll be out there looking for your daughter," said Leo. "However, do be aware I may not find her. I'll need to be paid either way."

Stockwell held on the cheque for a long uncomfortable moment and considered Leo through narrowed eyes. "Oh, you'll get paid," Stockwell finally said. "Don't worry about that."

14

"There's more to this than parliamentary expenses," Marcus Green said as he opened the folder and spread the papers across the desk. "He's clearly been fiddling the books for years, that's obvious. There's more to it than that. This goes deeper."

"What do you think?" the editor asked, scanning the information in front of him.

Green started to speak then stopped. The editor looked up, noticing the hesitation.

"You're in a safe space here, Marcus. You don't need the evidence just to tell me what you think. If you've got a theory, let's work it through. Get a couple of researchers on it, see if it has legs. If it doesn't, then we've lost nothing."

"It all started while I was investigating that robbery down in Brighton. Remember?" The editor nodded. "It was a professional job, and they only targeted one of the safety deposit boxes there. I mean, that's some restraint, as there must've been millions of pounds worth of god knows what in the others."

The editor flicked his hand for Green to get to the point.

"Because of the type of place it is, there's no record of what's in the boxes and nothing was ever recovered."

"What's this got to do with —"

"I couldn't match a name to the box that was stolen, but I managed to find out the bank account associated with it."

The editor's eyebrows rose.

"Here's a statement from that account."

"How did...?"

"Don't ask," Green said. "A contact. Look at this. A payment was made into the account every month. A large payment." Green slid his finger across the number. "And guess who that money comes from..."

Green and the editor shared a grin.

"Stockwell?"

"Exactly," Green said.

"Could be a coincidence?"

"In normal circumstances, I'd say yes," Green admitted. "But then the payments stopped."

"When?" the editor asked, looking up at the journalist.

"The week of the robbery."

15

Chimini crossed between the skeletal trees of the square and glanced up at the guesthouse. The building shone bright amid the long shadows of the late afternoon sun. She smiled. The place had started to feel like home.

She pulled a key from her pocket and held it toward the door. The cool metal felt important and hopeful. It was the first time she'd ever had a key to anything. She slid the key into the lock, pushed open the door and stepped inside.

The last few weeks had been a whirlwind. Finding the place, negotiating with the owner, and finally getting the keys. Now all they needed was the furniture. Then the guesthouse could support themselves and anyone else in need.

"Mānisakō, Mānisakō, Mānisakō."

Chimini closed the door and the rumble of city muted behind the glass. She heard an unusual noise and stopped.

"Mānisakō, Mānisakō, Mānisakō."

It came from nearby.

"Mānisakō."

It was a female voice. Nothing more than a whisper.

Chimini tried the door to the ground floor guesthouse. That was locked.

Then she saw movement under the stairs.

"Mānisakō."

Chimini peered into the gap beneath the stairs. A girl sat against the wall, her hands placed behind her head. She rocked gently forwards and backwards.

"Mānisakō," she whispered to herself.

"Hello?" Chimini said. "Are you okay?"

The girl didn't reply, but allowed Chimini to help her up.

"You'll be safe here. What are you doing here?"

The girl looked at Chimini with large, dark eyes. She said nothing.

"Let's go up," Chimini said, starting towards the stairs. "We will sit down and see if we can help you."

"Mānisako?"

"No, there are no men there. Just Allissa and me."

"Allissa?" the girl questioned, taking a step towards Chimini. "I have met Allissa."

"That's great then. You already know what to expect. Come on."

ALLISSA CHECKED THE ROOMS, the bathrooms and the storage spaces. Now she was running out of ideas. If the girl had left, had gone outside and run away, there wasn't much she could do.

Allissa crouched to look beneath the final bed. Nothing. Empty. The girl would be a few streets away by now. Allissa sat down and grumbled. Kathmandu was a dangerous place for vulnerable women. That's why she was setting up this guesthouse. It was supposed to be a safe place for those who desperately needed it — not a place they'd run away from.

Allissa rubbed her hands across her eyes. She hoped the girl had found somewhere safe to go. It hurt to see someone who needed help leave. They couldn't help everyone, though. That was never going to be possible.

Allissa heard voices coming from the reception area. *Chimini must be home.* Allissa listened closely and heard Chimini talking to someone in the tonal rhythms of Chimini's native Nepalese.

"Allissa?" Chimini called out.

"In here," Allissa called back.

"I found this young lady downstairs." Chimini appeared at the door with the girl beside her.

Allissa smiled and exhaled with relief.

"This is our guesthouse," Allissa explained once they were sat around the table in their small kitchen a few minutes later. "Chimini and I live here. There used to be another girl, but she got her own place last week. She'll be coming back to help us when we get up and running."

Fuli nodded.

"How long have you been in Kathmandu?" Allissa asked.

"I do not know," Fuli said, staring blankly.

Allissa reached across the table and touched Fuli's hand. Fuli turned and looked at Allissa.

"You're going to be safe here," Allissa said. "You can stay as long as you need."

16

O ne of the wonderful things about living by the sea are the sunsets. Particularly on the white-fronted terraces that line Brighton's streets. The buildings reflect every strand of pink and orange and turquoise that the sinking sun projects as it drags itself beneath the horizon.

On an occasional evening, when the banks of clouds have congealed across the rambling city, you think there'll be no sunset. Sometimes on these evenings, something special happens. At the last minute, the flailing sun passes a crease in the cloud and pours light through. It bounces over the sea and across the white-fronted buildings with their closed windows and wet slate tiles before disappearing again as quickly as it came.

After meeting with Stockwell and agreeing to go to Kathmandu, Leo needed to run more than ever.

The nervous part of him didn't want to go to Kathmandu at all. It didn't want to go anywhere. That cowardly part wanted to grovel for his job back and sit behind the safe glare of his computer screens. That way, he knew what he was dealing with. He didn't have to come up against people he didn't trust and places he didn't know.

Yet, Stockwell had given him ten thousand pounds, just as a down payment.

Leo looked out over the sea and tried to think of a time he'd made a decision like this before. His mind drew a blank. He couldn't think of one single occasion when he had actually decided to do anything for himself.

Leo knew that, to an extent, his lifestyle was a decision. He'd rejected the graduate schemes, pension plans and homeownership ideals of many people his age. But, that felt as if it were the way things had turned out — not a decision he'd made.

He wasn't even sure how he'd ended up being a journalist. Sure, he'd read a lot, and he liked writing. But that was a tiny part of his half political, half promotional job at *The Echo*.

Was this trip to Kathmandu his opportunity to do something different?

The thought filled Leo with excitement. He now had something to plan, something to sort. He'd have to book flights, arrange accommodation, research the city, and come up with ideas for what he was going to do when he got there.

And yet, he had no idea how to find anyone. He didn't know the language, the local customs, the places that someone might visit in Kathmandu. He'd never been there himself. Even if he planned it all, the idea of being successful was impossible to believe. It was all so far removed from the darkening promenade that it felt like a dream.

Who was he to think he could do this? This wasn't a job for some out-of-work journalist. Yes, he knew a little bit about finding people. And yet, so far he hadn't found anyone.

At that moment, an inch above the horizon, the sun broke through a crack in the clouds. Leo looked toward it as the sky filled with light. Every eddy and bump of the swirling grey glimmered in the dying light. Even the gulls streaking above sparkled as they cut through the low hanging clouds.

Leo narrowed his eyes to slits against the spray and pushed harder along the promenade.

Whether he had anxiety or not, whether it got him closer to Mya or not, this was his decision. Maybe the first real decision he'd ever made.

With stinging legs and the cold, wet air of winter filling his lungs, Leo knew he was going to Kathmandu.

17

"Let me tell you about home," Allissa's mother says, looking at the child she's just tucked in for the night. Allissa knows there's no feeling of safety quite like it.

"Home is different for everyone." Her mother's voice takes on the warm tones of her Kenyan accent. "But for me, it's where I grew up. I'll take you there one day."

Allissa looks up and their eyes lock.

"I think," her mother says, her voice slowing, "that it's the most beautiful place in the world. The sky is so big and blue you can't even imagine where it ends, and the land stretches for miles in every direction. In the distance you'll see mountains." She points across the room. Her eyes half close. "Right there, just their white peaks above the trees. When I was a child we played outside all day. We went down to the river where fresh strawberries grew from orange earth. They sprouted up, hundreds of them in great bushes, and we grabbed fistfuls of them." Her hands are alive now; they grab and squeeze the fruit of the past. "We'd have the juice running from our hands before washing them

49

in the river. By the river, the snails would live, bigger than an adult's fist." The hands reconstitute themselves into fists. "We would play there all day. One day my love..." — she looks down at the child whose eyes have now closed — "one day I'll take you there, and you'll know where my home is."

She kisses Allissa gently on the forehead and tucks the blanket tight. The night is late and hot. It's time to get some rest.

"But the thing is, as much as I want to share it with you, home is something you have to find for yourself."

———

"GOODNIGHT GIRLS," Allissa said as Chimini and Fuli left her in the kitchen. They'd offered to help with the clearing up, but Allissa liked the idea of doing it alone. It had been a busy day, fraught and hot. Some time spent on her own would be welcome.

"Allissa," Fuli said, turning at the door, "thank you."

"No problem. Sleep well," Allissa replied through a smile.

Allissa turned to the sink and looked out at the city through the window. In the next building, bright lights shone on a family sitting down to eat together. Allissa watched them as she filled the sink with water. The water heater on the wall clunked, the sound deep and metallic. In the last two years, Allissa had travelled through countless cities in numerous countries, but the smiles she saw as families ate together were always the same. It was a smile like no other; warm and familiar, embued with something else, something more.

As the sink filled, bubbles rising, Allissa thought of her family. The bubbles popped against her skin as she remembered her mother's hands. They were the first hands to hold her, the hands that fed and comforted, the hands that first introduced her to the world across which she'd now travelled tens of thousands of miles.

Allissa felt a wave of jealousy as she looked at the people in the next building. They had something she longed for so much — that connection with each other. Although she'd now travelled tens of thousands of miles, Allissa feared that connection may always be out of reach.

18

The first thing Leo noticed about Kathmandu was the taste. It rushed into the plane as the door swung open on the sweating tarmac of the airport. Leo didn't like it. It tasted like disaster and misery, pain and insecurity. Yet he knew that to the million residents of the mountain city, it was the smell of opportunity.

Flying in across the Kathmandu Valley, Leo had peered nervously from the bouncing plane. Below, the sprawling city was surrounded by snowcapped mountains in all directions. From the air, it looked as though the whole place was sinking into boggy earth.

Leo found the sheer scale of the city daunting. So was the idea he was looking for someone who may not be here. He needed to look all the same.

Leo's long flight across continents had started multiple number of hours ago at London Gatwick. He'd queued next to a pale, dreadlocked man who looked totally out of place in the modern veneer of the terminal.

Harbouring an innate fear of missing flights, he'd arrived many hours early. Unable to find anywhere to sit,

Leo pushed his bag against a wall and lowered himself on top of it. Next to him, a quick-fingered Asian man packed and repacked the same suitcase. The operation was supervised by two women who muttered comments Leo didn't understand yet was sure weren't helpful.

Now, pushing through the noisy, humid, tussle and scrum of the airport's exit, the part of Leo that wanted to go home screamed louder than ever. The threat of the unknown, looming large and fearful, weighed on his mind while the straps of his backpack cut into his shoulders. He would just have to get out amongst the lives and experiences of people in the city. He would have to ask questions and likely chase many shadows in pursuit of Allissa Stockwell.

Leo opened the door of a taxi, pushed his bag inside and climbed in beside it, never letting go of the straps. The taxi, a pink and white hatchback, was covered with dust. The green digital clock on the dash informed him it was five in the afternoon. To Leo, it felt like the middle of the night. He supposed probably it was. He needed to find his hotel and eat proper food on solid ground. Then he'd get some sleep.

"To The Best Kathmandu Guesthouse," Leo said. The driver examined him in the rearview mirror without responding.

"The, Best, Kathmandu, Guesthouse," Leo said again, slowly. The driver tilted his head to the side.

Leo exhaled. This was going to be more difficult than he'd anticipated.

"The... Best..." he started, sounding each word as though his pronunciation was at fault.

The driver snapped the flimsy gear stick forward, kicked the accelerator, and sent the car screeching from the kerb. Leo fell backward into the worn seats and looked around for the seatbelt and buckle.

The pitch and ferocity of the engine grew until it sounded as though it were on the brink of explosion. Leo peered up from the back seat. At the end of the slip road, a wall of traffic sneered. The driver's knuckles whitened against the steering wheel and his head whipped from side to side.

Engines screeched as horns screamed.

A gap in the traffic appeared, and the driver accelerated for it. The vibrations of the car became violent. With another cacophony of horns, they slipped into the gap with inches to spare. The driver braked to avoid the car in front, and Leo slid down into the footwell.

He scrambled back up to the seat and checked for the seatbelt again. He couldn't find one.

Kathmandu looked the same from the car as it had from the air. An ungainly, untidy concrete mass of buildings. Each one was no higher than a few storeys, but seemingly endless in their number.

What couldn't be seen from the plane, though it was obvious to Leo now, was the life that inhabited the city. Every inch of the city was alive, an organic mass of moving, working parts. Each tiny shop or business spilled out into the street; welders, mechanics, and what looked like a pot maker spinning clay on a wheel.

The traffic engulfed the taxi. Lorries overladen with bulging loads, people leaning from the pushed out windows of buses, donkeys pulling carts. Amongst them all, an army of pink and white taxis honked and revved.

Having visited India with Mya, Leo thought he was prepared for Kathmandu. But doing it on his own was different. This time he had a job to do. He would have to go where the trail took him, whether he wanted to or not.

The doubts swarmed his cluttered mind. How would he

know who to trust? What if the taxi driver took him to the wrong place? What if someone tried to rob him? Tourists were known to carry lots of cash, and Leo's pale complexion made him appear more inexperienced than most. Leo's fists tightened. He could probably overpower the small driver, but if the driver knew other people — of course he knew other people — Leo knew he wouldn't stand a chance.

His chest tightened.

Breathing quickened.

Calm, focus, breathe.

Leo needed to bring it under control.

Breathe in.

And out.

In.

Leo thought of Mya and the taxi ride they'd shared from the airport in Mumbai — Leo's first experience of India. They'd come through a similar scrum and into the wet heat of the Indian summer. In that first taxi ride from the airport, Leo felt as if he'd learned more about the diversity of human existence than ever before. The brand new airport terminal of marble and chrome surrounded by sprawling slums of glinting shacks. The seemingly disconnected images: cars, lorries, bikes, a motorway. Cows, chickens, pigs. Children playing. Men working. Women working. People washing in pots on the side of the road, then relieving themselves next to those same pots. Making breakfast. Or, just sitting and watching the world fly by.

He was amazed at the spectacle. Proud that he was there, guilty he lived in such an opulent way by comparison. Shame he didn't appreciate it, fear that it was all so different. Then, he felt Mya's hand on the seat between them. Her fingers knitted with his. With that came comfort, reliability and the knowledge that things would be alright.

The taxi moved to the right of the carriageway and stopped violently. A discord of horns sounded from the surrounding vehicles. Gravel skittered and pinged.

The taxi driver's small, dark hands gripped the wheel. The driver pulled himself forward on the seat and fixed his eyes on a slow-moving truck heading toward them. Fifty metres away. It blocked the traffic on the narrow street. Thirty metres. Leo stared into its vast silver grill. Ornately painted figures of gods and demons covered the truck's body. Twenty metres. The driver revved the engine to a furious squeal. Fifteen. The taxi lurched forward, hard to the right. Dust. The sound of horns and tyres, rubber slipping on dirt roads.

Leo caught his breath as the car spun forwards. Kathmandu whirled past the windows. The driver shouted in exhilaration.

Leo closed his eyes.

Horns. Shouts. Tyres screamed. The car whirled one-hundred and eighty degrees. Then all was still.

Then, they began to move in the opposite direction. Leo opened his eyes. The driver had pulled them into a tiny gap between the slow-moving truck and an overloaded minibus and they were now heading back the way they'd come.

Leo's chest felt stabbed by invisible needles. His lungs clawed for air.

Breathe in.

And out.

Then, and with no indication, the driver stopped at the side of the road. A deep horn resonated from the lorry behind as it slowed to pass.

The driver paid no attention. He left the car with its engine whining and ran into a shop.

Leo waited. Anxiety bubbled through his chest. Is this

where the driver got his friends to come and rob the helpless tourist? Leo thought of running. He could grab his bag and go.

He didn't know where he was. There was no way he'd find the hotel from here. He needed to stay. At least to see what happened.

The door of the shop swung open and the driver returned. Behind him walked another man. A big man. Leo felt panic rise further. This was the biggest Nepalese man he'd seen.

Leo focused on his breathing.

The big man towered over the taxi driver. His hair was cut short, and his thick neck must have been the size of Leo's waist. His arms swung dangerously at his sides. The taxi driver pointed towards the car and Leo.

Leo watched through the panic and helplessness.

Breathe in and out.

He focused on his breathing. He needed to suppress the panic.

The rear door of the taxi flew open.

Breathe in.

The big man leaned in toward Leo.

Breathe out.

The big man filled the door.

Leo sat helplessly. *Breathe in.*

Traffic surged past the right of the taxi. Each vehicle, only inches from the passenger door. The was no way Leo could get out there.

Breathe out.

The big man pushed himself further into the car.

Why did I even come? This was a terrible idea.

Leo tried to think of home. The image of his tattered flat and unemployment brought him no reassurance.

"You, ah, looki, for a 'otel?" the big man said in raspy, broken English. "Your 'otel?" he repeated.

Slowly the realization dawned.

"You lookin for 'otel?"

"Yes," Leo said. The big man was trying to help the taxi driver understand him.

Between gasps, Leo told the man the name of his hotel. The big man barked the translation to the taxi driver, who nodded and leapt back into the car. The driver sunk back into the seat and the big man lumbered back into his shop. Next time Leo would have to bring the hotel's address in writing.

The taxi driver snapped the flimsy car into gear and revved into the stream of traffic and dust.

19

Ten days had elapsed between Leo's meeting with Stockwell in the Grand Hotel on Brighton seafront and the moment he walked through the doors of The Best Kathmandu Guesthouse. Standing in the gloomy, cavernous foyer, Leo realised the two could not have been more different. One exhibited brass details, crystal chandeliers and thick carpets. The other, an ill-fitting door which let a stream of dust run across the tiles and an old television fizzing intermittently between two channels.

Leo had booked The Best Kathmandu Guesthouse three days ago. He'd wanted to be sparing with money, and despite the suspicious name, The Best Kathmandu Guest-house was cheap. Although Stockwell's cheque now rested in Leo's bank account, he didn't know if he would ever see the next payment. The fact he didn't have a job on his return was constantly on his mind.

Leo had also researched Kathmandu. He wanted to try and understand what would bring a twenty-eight year old woman here. What he found was a thriving, historic city steeped in Buddhist and Hindu history. Several sacred temples and monasteries had stood resolute through the change of centuries and empires, and withstood many earthquakes. Leo made a note to visit these places if he had the chance. *It would be a shame to miss the culture,* he'd thought in a uncharacteristic surge of positivity.

Leo wanted to know who he was working for. Stockwell had been a Member of Parliament until his appointment to the House of Lords five years ago. Hailing from a wealthy family, he'd attended the most reputable schools and universities, where he'd taken an interest in politics.

"Welcome to The Best Kathmandu Guesthouse," came a voice from behind the reception desk. "A nice day I am wishing you." A man in an immaculate brown uniform smiled at Leo. Leo returned the greeting as energetically as he could.

After completing the check-in process, involving Leo's details being manually entered into a large ledger, the receptionist carried Leo's bag up to his room. The man reached the room on the sixth floor without breaking a sweat. Despite carrying nothing, Leo was out of breath. After dropping the bag on the bed the receptionist turned on the ceiling fan, mimed the use of the bathroom, then let himself out. As his footsteps drew away, Leo sat down and looked around the modest room. It was a museum piece of eighties design in green and yellow.

The journey had been long and arduous, but Leo had made it to Kathmandu. His arrival, however, had brought little relief. His work would now begin.

Leo lay back on the lumpy mattress, shut his eyes, and tried to ignore images of the taxi drivers, uneaten plane food and inescapable waiting rooms that began to drift through his mind.

20

"But how come the princess always ends up with some man at the end?" Chimini asked, closing the book on the table of the guesthouse's small kitchen.

"That's just how these stories go," Allissa said, stirring the steaming pot and adding more turmeric.

"Are they saying it is important to have a guy to be happy? I don't think there are any princes in Kathmandu."

"You don't need to think about it in that much detail," Allissa said, turning from the stove. "I just saw the books in market and thought of you. Not because you love princes, but because you might want something to practise reading in English."

Chimini looked through the pile of brightly-coloured books on the table and muttered to Fuli sitting beside her. Allissa had been helping Chimini improve her English over the last few months, but reading it was still a challenge.

"Well, if that is the case, I need to get you something to read in Nepalese." Chimini smiled.

"Yes, definitely," Allissa said, turning back to the food to hide her frown. The thought of reading the curved script of Nepali writing felt like climbing a mountain. "I'd love to," she said, gazing into the bubbling liquid.

Chimini flicked through a different book with colourful pictures. She held it up so Fuli could see. "In this one, the princess looks so unhappy until the prince comes along. Miserable! Like there is nothing to her life. It is..." She searched for the word.

"Boring?"

"Yes, it looks like she is very bored before she meets this man."

"Well, if you don't like them..." Allissa said, beaming at the women.

"No, no, I like them. I am just wondering, where is the one where the princess gets so bored of bad men she thinks life on her own is better?"

"Well, let's write our own," Allissa said, stifling a laugh as Chimini translated for Fuli. "The food is ready, I think."

Neither girl responded. Chimini's eyes darted from Allissa to the books. Her mouth hidden behind the palm of her hand as she whispered to Fuli. Fuli's face melted into a smile.

"What are you saying about me?" Allissa said, pointing the wooden spoon toward them.

"Nothing!" Chimini replied, whispering again. Fuli laughed.

"Tell me now, or there'll be trouble." Allissa took on the deep voice of a fairy tale villain.

"No, I will never tell you!" Chimini shouted, feigning fear, then winking at Fuli. "We will never tell you..."

"Right, that's it..." Allissa took a step toward the giggling women.

"Okay... okay..." Chimini said, recovering herself from the fit of laughter. "We think you are the princess."

Shrieks and laughs echoed through the guesthouse as beyond their sanctuary, Kathmandu slipped into restless darkness.

Residents scuttled home passing tourists on the way to the city's bars and restaurants. Tourists who may have heard the legend of the restaurant advertised only by the bare bulb. They may be making their way down the warren of reducing passages already.

They may be hoping to try the Himalayan Lamb.

21

As Marcus Green drove home, he turned the things he knew through his mind. It had been a successful meeting with the newspaper's editor. As a freelance journalist, Green was used to working alone. The fact that this editor was offering resources to help him proved the scale of the story.

For the first ten miles of the busy motorway, Green weaved his BMW between cruising cars. As the novelty of speed wore off and his thoughts became more and more preoccupied with the case, he slowed into the second lane.

It was an interesting case. Something was going on. Something wasn't right. Every sense Green had convinced him it was something big.

He knew Stockwell had made payments every month to the unknown account. There was nothing wrong with that. It was mysterious, but not illegal. People paid for all sorts of things. But for those payments to stop the same week as the robbery, and the only safety deposit box affected to be one linked to the account... That was suspicious.

Green needed to know what was in the box. That was

the key to this. Was it something Stockwell wanted? Or was it something he wanted to keep hidden?

Traffic started to slow and a sea of strobing brake lights appeared ahead. Time was going to be key with this case. Stockwell was a powerful man, and powerful men could always find ways to keep their secrets hidden.

Green had learned how dangerous his job could be a few months ago while investigating a businessman suspected of laundering money through a non-league football team. It happened after a two month investigation, the night before the story was set to be published. Green was driving home, much like today. Back then he'd never expected to see the figure on the backseat of his car. He never checked before setting off. Now he checked every day.

The figure had stayed hidden as Green drove from the car park. His mind was on other things. He remembered it clearly. It was not until he was driving down a dark lane near his house that he felt the cold metal on his throat and saw the dark shadow in the rearview mirror.

Green pulled to a stop and felt his neck where the knife had pierced the skin. His fingers traced where the slow trickle of blood ran beneath his collar.

Green ran the story anyway, but on the day it was published he went to stay with friends in Liverpool for a month. After returning home he hadn't seen or heard anything from the man. Yet, he still continued to check the back seat of the car, and even had security cameras and an alarm system installed in his house.

Stockwell, if Green had him right, was equally powerful and equally dangerous. Building the case around him would have to be done carefully. A threat could come from anywhere. He would have to be vigilant.

One thing he knew, Stockwell wouldn't go down without a fight.

22

Leo awoke in the dark the following morning. He was disorientated. At first he thought he must have shut the curtains before going to sleep. Then he noticed the city's glow from behind the glass. The sun hadn't risen yet. He lay on his back and watched the morning creep across the sky.

He estimated it must have been around seven in the evening when he arrived at the hotel. He'd been awake for over thirty-six hours, though, so he couldn't be sure. As to what time it was now, he couldn't even guess.

He crossed the room and pulled his phone from his bag. He entered the passcode and the phone lit up. It was just before six in the morning. He'd been asleep for nearly twelve hours. An icon flashed, showing the receipt of four text messages. Two network messages detailed the cost of phone use in Nepal; in summary, loads. Another from Stockwell asked if there was any progress on the investigation. One from his Mum wished him a good flight. Leo felt guilty reading the message from his mum. He'd only called two days ago to say that he was going to Kathmandu. He thought about not saying anything, but decided his folks should know where he was. He made it sound positive though — "a great opportunity" — though he hadn't even convinced himself yet that were true.

"What, you've been given the time off work?" his mum asked, reminding him he'd not even told them about losing his job. The lies made him feel worse, but he knew they wouldn't understand.

Leo drew a deep breath and looked out at the restless city. There was something reassuring about it being behind the glass, even though Leo knew he would soon have to face it. He was going to have to go out there. Maybe, somewhere in this city, this sprawling expanse of life and love and pain and money, was the girl he sought.

An hour later, Leo wearily descended the six flights of stairs. Today he planned to get over the jet lag and begin to orientate himself. Getting a feeling for the place was going to be important. He needed to try and get to know the city if he was to understand why a young woman would come here. Tomorrow the search would begin with a visit to the bank where Allissa had withdrawn the money.

Leo stood in the hotel's foyer and gulped a deep and calming breath. Behind the door, through the pane of dirt-smeared glass, thick traffic rumbled. Leo released the air and let his shoulders relax. Then he pushed open the door and stepped out into the madness.

Traffic seethed around him. Bikes, taxis, carts and cars all wrestled for space on the thin road. Ahead, an over-loaded lorry squeezed past a man pulling a cart laden with bricks. A mule's legs buckled beneath bags of cement.

Leo drew a breath of the thin air. It was filled with the fumes of passing traffic, the dust of the city, and laced with his own anxiety of the unknown. It brought on a tightness in his chest.

Breathe. Focus and breathe.

In a moment of panic, Leo glanced back at the door. His hotel room would bring him no peace. The only thing to do was to get out into the city and settle in.

Leo took a moment to focus on the street around him and let his breathing slow down. He needed to stay calm. Each breath was rough on his throat. He looked to the right and tried to make out the marketplace which the map said was just a short walk away. That's where he was going to start.

Leo took another deep, calming breath. Then he set off.

23

Allissa awoke to the sound of Chimini and Fuli chatting. She sat up in bed and checked the time. She'd slept late. The morning light was already spilling in through the window, which reminded her they still needed to buy curtains.

With a sudden flurry of contentment, she remembered the alarms which used to ring between five and six am in her family home. There was none of that here. Now she ran on her own time.

She rubbed her eyes and thought about what they needed to do today. It was essential they sorted furniture for the other rooms. She didn't want to have to turn people away when they arrived wanting to stay in the guesthouse. Fuli's unexpected arrival demonstrated how essential a place like this was in the city.

The dream Allissa and Chimini shared was to make the guesthouse a viable business so that it could provide a safe place to work and live for young women like Fuli. It would teach them skills, build their confidence, and help them make a success of their lives.

Allissa didn't need to hear Fuli's story to know what she had been through. She knew of the gangs of men who visited the remote and impoverished villages of Nepal, where they promised young women exciting jobs in the city. Jobs which became forced prostitution, with no possible return to the homes they'd left behind.

24

Fifteen minutes later Leo cradled a steaming mug of coffee. He sat at the window of a small café, nestled next to a shop that sold the sort of keepsakes and talismans that people visiting Asia collected by the bucket-load. He watched, sipping from his drink as the shop owner lined up model Buddhas in bronze or wood, fat and thin, a face either beaming with an enlightened smile or a look of peaceful stillness.

It wasn't until Leo saw the café's menu that the idea of food really crossed his mind. He hadn't eaten properly since leaving the UK. On arrival in Kathmandu, fatigue had been his first concern. With that need now met, his stomach rumbled.

Across the road, market sellers unloaded fruit and vegetables from trolleys and carts. Leo had visited markets in Asia before, but still found himself smiling in fascination at the vibrancy of it all. He watched one man arrange his tomatoes in a pyramid, each a slightly different tone on the red-green spectrum. Another opened sacks of spices, which he laid carefully around a large pestle and mortar. At the edge of the market, almost opposite Leo, a man created bright garlands of flowers. Leo watched him threading yellow and orange petals on a string with a large needle.

A truck pulled to a stop and sounded its horn. The driver gestured wildly. The man making the garlands gave three to a small boy, who ran across and handed them up to the driver. A few coins were passed down in payment and the truck lumbered off, the garlands swinging from its rearview mirror.

Opposite the café, a man raised a metal shutter to reveal a travel agency. Posters of lakes and mountains adorned the windows, hinting at the Nepalese beauty beyond the grimy, sweating city. Leo knew Allissa could have left Kathmandu. Buses to other towns, cities or countries were cheap and frequent, and kept no records of the passengers they took. If Allissa had boarded one of these, there was very little Leo could do. She would be lost to him. Without reason, Leo found the thought saddening. He wanted to find her. Not just for the money. For the answers.

Of course, a positive report to Stockwell would be well-received. Leo remembered the text message from Stockwell that had arrived during the night. He dug out his phone and tapped a reply.

Arrived in Kathmandu, beginning search, will keep you informed.

A young tourist couple crossed the road and examined the display of Buddhas and flags outside the shop. The couple were tanned, blonde-haired and wore baggy, loose-fitting trousers with pictures of elephants printed across them. The shop keeper fussed around, polishing any item they took an interest in with an oily rag until it gleamed. The girl picked up a bronze statue of the Buddha sitting peacefully and turned to look at her partner.

Leo and Mya had been travelling like that some years ago. Travelling just to see, to experience, and to enjoy. Anxiety hadn't bothered him then. With Mya, he took it all in his stride.

A ring glinted from the young woman's finger. Something in the way she wore it suggested to Leo it was new to her. Perhaps the tanned, muscular man presented her with it just days ago.

Leo brooded over the dregs of his coffee.

Without realizing what he was doing, Leo picked up his phone and scrolled to a picture of Mya. It didn't take long. He had an album of them which he needed to keep for the search.

It was the most recent photograph of her he'd taken before she disappeared. She looked toward a crystal blue ocean. Her wide eyes squinted against the sun. Her skin was bronzed and her hair was dark and luxuriant. Like he had many times before, Leo wished their holiday had ended differently. If only he'd had the confidence to do it earlier. To say it, to ask her... Then at least he'd know her answer.

The couple wandered in the direction of the market, her hand firmly re-planted in his. The ring glimmered, as did their smiles.

25

As usual the city pulsed as Allissa and Chimini picked their way along the road toward the market. Chimini was taking them to a shop which she thought sold the furniture they needed. Buying anything in Kathmandu was both a social and business process. Neither sellers nor buyers rushed the negotiation, which often included chai and a long but essential conversation about every member of their family.

"It's up here," Chimini said. "Past the market, then on the right."

Walking anywhere in Kathmandu was not an easy task. The sides of the roads were badly maintained, and the traffic swerved and swooped without regard for the plight of pedestrians. The holy cows had it slightly better. But only slightly.

All around them, shop keepers, tradesmen and stall-holders began the daily ritual of providing for their families. Allissa knew, however simple their lives were, however apparent it might be that they would never leave the city, they were the lucky ones. They had the security of habit and a family to provide for. It wasn't necessarily about who you needed, but about who needed you.

"Just up here," Chimini said, walking in front of Allissa. "A couple of minutes past the market. I saw it yesterday."

Allissa nodded in reply. She only heard every other word against the growling traffic. A young couple walked hand in hand ahead of them. A small plastic bag dangled from the man's free hand. Allissa imagined the far-off relative who, on receipt of a laughing Buddha, would laugh too before sliding it into a drawer full of other foreign novelties.

Sure enough, there was a gift stall across the road. Beside it a beaming shopkeeper counted a wad of greasy notes. The café next door spilled the fragrance of ground coffee into the street. Coffee in Kathmandu was good.

"I'm going to get us coffee," Allissa shouted. Chimini carried on walking toward the market. "I'm going to..." Allissa shouted again, startling an old lady bent double carrying a bucket of onions. This time the sound of her voice was dwarfed by a passing truck, the thug of its diesel engine straining against the heavy load. Chimini disappeared between the stalls. Allissa knew that if they lost sight of each other in there it could take ages to find each other again. She shook her head and walked on. Coffee would have to wait.

26

In the restaurant, two men prepare for the evening's service. They know it will be busy; it always is. Their customers will arrive, following the directions of someone who knew someone. Their restaurant is talked about as part of Kathmandu legend.

The restaurant is invisible by day, without the hanging bulb illuminating the way. The bulb which each traveller, hoping to try the Himilayan Lamb, will pass below.

In the restaurant's kitchen, buried deep within the building, the two men prepare the meat. Sharp knives glint as they slice skin from flesh, flesh from bone. Foreheads prickle with perspiration as ovens are lit and spices are added.

Each man knows preparation is key. The cut, the spice, the heat.

The phone on the wall of the kitchen rings. One of the men puts down the knife and goes to answer it. His fingers are bloodstained.

The voice on the other end is far away. It's the call

they've been expecting. They have a special job to do in the next day or so.

27

Leo returned to his hotel in the early evening. He found navigating the city by day difficult enough, so wanted to get back before dark. The day had been tiring, and he wanted an early night to refresh for his search to begin in earnest the following morning. He'd spent most of the afternoon watching locals barter over colourful fruit, or excitable tourists browse row upon row of statues, fabrics or flags. The diesel, dust and altitude of the city had made his breathing heavy, even from the short walk.

Sitting in a cafe, it had impressed upon Leo how possible it was that he and Allissa could just pass in the chaotic street. While travelling with Mya, they'd seen a guy she knew in India. She'd not seen him for years, yet there he was, walking down the same street, at the same time as they were. Coincidences like that were possible, Leo knew, as his eyes scanned the bustling crowds.

Leo planned to spend the evening reviewing all his research on Allissa and her family. He'd bought numerous snacks and a pack of Everest Beers on the way back to the hotel.

He took out the photos and laid them across the bed, examining each one carefully. He wanted to try and think of Allissa as a friend. He didn't know why, possibly just a streak of unusual optimism, but somehow he thought she was close. Leo knew Allissa could have left the city, got on any one of the buses that pulled out into the mountains every day. But why would she need all that money?

Laying the final two photos on the bed cover, Leo stepped back and snapped the top from one of the Everest Beers. He glanced at the can. The blue label depicted a mountain climber on a snow covered slope.

He took a sip and examined the assembled photographs. All the information he had on the Stockwells told of a hard-working, well-educated and wealthy family. They seemed completely devoid of argument, incident or public embarrassment. Almost too devoid of it. It was as though their reputation had been carefully stage-managed.

Leo scanned the pictures for anything hinting to a different story. It was interesting how, compared with the other Stockwell children, Allissa wasn't photographed often at all. Leo swigged the beer and picked up one of the photographs. Stockwell presented a trophy to a small man in a jockey's outfit. Behind them, a glossy-coated horse looked dazed. Archie and Lucy stood at their father's feet. They were young children and grinned up at the camera. Leo guessed that Archie must have been around eight in the picture, meaning Lucy was around five, and Allissa two or three. *Why isn't Allissa there?*

He replaced the photo and scanned the collection again. His eyes came to rest on a family photo which included

Allissa. It looked as though it had been taken quite recently. The five members of the family stood in a well-manicured garden, most likely their Berkshire family home. Lord and Lady Stockwell stood in the centre and the three children to the sides, Archie to the right, Lucy and Allissa to the left. Lucy and Archie both had clear family resemblance; the reddened face, thick-set bodies and deep, intense eyes. Allissa was different. She didn't wear the contrived smiles of the others and glanced off to the right of the photographer. She was slender, dark-skinned, and her face was lit with a naturally bright expression. Her hair curled, loose and large, hinting at an African heritage. The only logical explanation, Leo supposed, tapping the edge of the picture, was that she had a different mother.

Leo spent an evening trying to find out who Allissa's mother was. There was scant public information about Allissa Stockwell as it was, let alone her mother. Allissa had just appeared in the family around twenty years ago. Of course, it could be a coincidence, one with a perfectly reasonable and logical explanation. Leo doubted it. There was a mystery here. Instinct told Leo that Blake Stockwell wanted it to stay that way.

Leo looked at the picture again. It gave him the impression that Allissa's appearance wasn't the only thing separating her from the others. The way Allissa gazed absently away made it look as though she wanted to be somewhere else. Without knowing why, Leo thought of his own family. He remembered a meal they'd shared two weeks ago, a time when he still had a job and knew nothing of Allissa, Lord Stockwell or Kathmandu. Surrounded by the coos and squeals of his two-year-old nephew, Leo had listened to talk of his sister and her husband's new house, how he should get a place of his own, and how they thought that still looking for Mya was a waste of time.

At that moment Leo felt as if he were the one looking out of the photograph. Physically he was there. Yet, he wanted to be somewhere else.

28

Allissa opened her eyes and took her first waking breath of the muggy Kathmandu morning. She knew the day would be special. It was the day that everything would come together and fall in to place. The day the planets aligned, and things worked out to make her dream come true.

When Allissa had arrived in Kathmandu a few months before she had known nothing of the plight of women like Chimini and Fuli. Women who had been lied to, imprisoned and abused, all for the pleasure of cruel and greedy men. She'd just been travelling the world with no real plan. No purpose. Just to see, and to experience. To not go home.

In those early Kathmandu days, Allissa wandered the dusty streets, seeing little to separate the manic city from many others across Asia. Sure, it had nice sites — temples, bazaars and the visible, heady curve of the mountain ridges — but there had been nothing to persuade her to stay. On what was supposed to be her final day, Allissa met a group of charity workers in a restaurant. The place was busy, and they invited her to join their table. They spoke of countries they'd visited, and adventures they'd had — in the way travellers do wherever they meet the world over. Then one young lady from Australia named Kate had told Allissa of the work they did.

They visited remote villages high in the mountains, days of travel from anywhere else, in order to spread the word about the gangs of men who also made the same journeys. Gangs who promised the village's young women jobs in the big city. Jobs which, when they arrived in the city, were nothing more than time spent on a soiled mattress in a dark room.

With the restaurant bustling around them, listening to tales of the work Kate and the team were doing, Allissa realised she'd been doing it all wrong. She'd been travelling the world looking for something she needed. Something she felt was missing. In fact, all that time she'd needed to find a way in which the world needed her. In Kate and the others around that table, Allissa had started to find it.

The conversations continued late into the night, and enthralled Allissa so much that she asked if she could join them on their next trip. She left Kathmandu two days later, along with three others: Kate, a young man from Canada, and a Nepalese girl called Chimini. For a month they'd travelled to some of the remotest parts of the country, visiting some of the poorest and most undeveloped villages. By the time they returned to Kathmandu, Allissa knew what she was going to do. Her dream had been formed. It was a dream which, with the arrival of the furniture for the guesthouse today, would finally be complete.

29

L eo winced as he stepped out into the Kathmandu morning. The traffic growled past, kicking up dust and fumes in the thin air which stung his eyes and burned his lungs. Leo knew he would have to get used to it. He was here for a few days yet. Maybe even weeks.

Leo saw the white and pink body of a taxi and held up a tentative arm. The taxi crunched to a stop beside him.

Learning from his experience of two days ago, Leo handed the driver a piece of paper which detailed the destination he required. He had a small stack of The Best Kathmandu Guesthouse's business cards for the return journey.

Ten minutes later, the taxi stopped outside the SNC Everest Bank. Leo paid the driver, got out and looked up at the bank's front door. It didn't look like the sort of place from which you could withdraw a small fortune. It didn't really look like they knew anything about money at all.

Like many of the businesses in Kathmandu, the bank occupied one unit on the ground floor of a four-storey concrete building. Except for the faded red and green sign, it was indistinguishable from the shops on either side. Sun-bleached posters taped to the inside of the glass advertised the services the bank offered: *ATM, International Money Transfer, and Safety Deposit Boxes.* This is where Allissa withdrew thirty-five-thousand dollars. She had been here. She had stood on the same pavement and looked up at the same sign. Leo was chasing a ghost. One thing he knew for certain was that they would have taken an address when Allissa collected the money. He needed that address.

Leo took a deep breath and tried to ignore his rising anxiety. Then he stepped into the bank.

The bank itself was nothing more than a small room, gloomy in comparison to the harsh, muggy daylight. Dust streaked across the floor and a faded ATM blinked from the shadows. A Nepalese lady spoke harshly on the phone behind the desk in the corner.

Leo approached the desk. The bank teller continued her conversation for several minutes before putting the phone down. It didn't sound like a business call. Leo imagined her scolding a child. Finally she spoke to Leo in Nepalese. Leo couldn't even decipher where one word ended and the next began, let alone understand their meaning.

"Do you speak English?" Leo asked hopefully. "I'm looking for my sister."

Leo decided his best option was pretend to be Allissa's brother. That way his interest was easily explained. Perhaps people would feel sorry for him.

His question elicited nothing but a blank look. Leo showed the most recent picture of Allissa. The teller peered at the picture through her dark-rimmed glasses. Leo thought he saw a flicker of recognition. Allissa was the sort of person someone would remember.

The lady spoke again.

"I don't understand," Leo said, his palms out in surrender. "I'm sorry."

"Manu," the lady shouted.

Leo straightened up.

"Manu," she shouted again.

There was no response. Leo looked nervously around the bank.

The woman stood suddenly and walked to the doorway which led into the shop's back room. She pulled a curtain of plastic strips aside and shouted through.

A distant male voice replied, followed by the sound of a chair scraping on tile.

Leo felt his anxiety rise as the gruff voice moved toward them. He turned and checked the door behind him. Traffic thudded past continuously.

"Hello, can I help?" said a man as he pushed through the curtain into the room. "My wife said" — he indicated the woman behind the desk with a wave — "you are looking for someone. How can I help?"

"Yes," Leo said. "My sister. I have a picture. She withdrew some money here two weeks ago."

The man leaned over and peered at the phone. Leo again watched for any sign of recognition. This time he saw none.

The man and woman had a short conversation. Leo couldn't work out if they agreed or not, or if they were going to help him.

"My wife says that yes, she was here. She did not think we should tell you that, but I do not see the harm. I am sorry to say we are not able to tell you any more."

"I'll pay," Leo said, pulling out a small bundle of notes. "If you can tell me the address my sister gave you, I'll pay."

The woman interjected with a torrent of words, pointing

at the money. Leo couldn't tell whether she was excited or insulted.

"No," the man said, holding his hand out to indicate the door. "We have a responsibility of secrecy to our clients. I have already said too much."

A rock formed in Leo's throat. He glanced at the door. To leave now would be to leave with nothing.

"Please." Leo knitted his fingers together and took a step forward. "You have to help me. My sister's in Kathmandu all alone. We're all worried about her. We've not seen or heard from her in years."

The man's arms dropped to his side. He looked from his wife to Leo and back again.

"I need to know where she is," Leo said, his pulse raging.

The man shifted his weight from one foot to the other.

"I'm sorry," he said.

"Do you have any children yourself?" Leo stepped to the side so that he could address both the man and the woman. "Imagine if they were lost on the other side of the world."

The man spoke to his wife. She replied sharply. He nodded.

"I'm sorry," he said, looking at the floor. "We cannot tell you anything about our customers. I wish you luck in finding your sister, but I can't do any more to help you."

"Please, you have to," Leo said, glancing from one stony face to the other.

The door swung open and a short woman bustled into the bank. Exhaust fumes and dust filled the room.

"No," the man said. "We have customers now, so you have to go." He pointed at the door. "I wish you luck and sorry we cannot help."

Leo sighed. That had been his only lead. The only thing

he knew about Allissa in Kathmandu. The bank had her address, but if they wouldn't give it to him, Leo didn't know how he could get it. He couldn't just demand it or steal it. He stepped out into the dazzling morning sun with nothing.

30

Allissa stood behind the guesthouse's small reception desk and watched two men carry furniture up the stairs. They'd brought only the frames of the beds in the first load; that was all their small truck would hold. They would return with the mattresses, dressing tables and wardrobes later. It was to be a full day's work for the men, who were already taking directions from Chimini about what was to go where.

Allissa looked around and realised she'd not seen Fuli for some time; perhaps she hadn't yet got up. Allissa crossed to Fuli's bedroom and looked inside. The blankets were piled on one side. The bed was empty.

Remembering how Fuli had run from the building the day before, Allissa felt a pang of alarm. *What if she's done that again? What if she slipped out while we were dealing with the delivery men? She could be anywhere by now.* At the far end of the reception area, the kitchen door stood open. Allissa rushed across the reception and into the kitchen.

Fuli was there, in the back corner, her hands covering her face.

Allissa turned back to the reception area and called to Chimini.

Chimini sat beside Fuli and spoke quietly to her. Allissa watched from the door, but couldn't hear what was said. Chimini helped Fuli to her feet and they crossed to the door, hand-in-hand.

"Look," Chimini said as the men lumbered up the stairs, "not all men are horrible."

31

Back in his hotel room, Leo ran over the events of the afternoon. He felt he'd done everything he could to get the address from the man and woman in the bank. He supposed if he really were Allissa's brother, knowing that she was alive and well would be reassuring. That wasn't enough. He had a job to do. He needed to find Allissa and report back.

Leo blinked. He'd spent the last two hours researching on his laptop via the hotel's frustrating Wi-Fi. His eyes and neck ached. On the pad in front of him he scrawled the addresses of hotels and guesthouses close to the bank. They would be his first stops tomorrow. Leo also needed to find someone who spoke Nepalese to help him.

Leo's stomach rumbled. He'd hardly eaten in the last few days. He put the laptop on the bed beside him and stretched, then crossed to the darkened window. He hadn't even noticed the light fade.

The weather had deteriorated throughout the afternoon. By the time Leo's taxi had cut through the busy streets on the way back to the hotel, burgeoning dark clouds had thickened on all sides. Moisture in the air promised rain that so far hadn't arrived. Beyond the window, the turbulent sky brooded. It matched Leo's mood.

Leo looked at the building behind The Best Kathmandu Guesthouse, bathed in the orange glow from the occasional streetlight and the misty swish of passing cars. It was unfinished, with steel ribs poking through some kind of plastic covering. Light danced and shone across its surface. Leo looked down and saw lines of swaying Chinese lanterns, suspended on cables above what looked like a restaurant.

Leo conceded to the grumbles of his stomach. Five minutes later, he crossed to an empty table at the back of the restaurant. Above chattering diners, scurrying waiters and the tumbling smell of spice and ginger, the Chinese lanterns he had seen from his room shimmered.

Sliding into one of the four chairs, Leo glanced around. The casual noise of conversation was calming, as was the idea that he didn't need to be part of it. Solitude was good.

"Don't eat too much," said a lady with a New York accent from the next table. "I wanna go to that restaurant later."

"Well yeah, but we might not find it, and I'm hungry now," replied the man opposite her, tearing into a flatbread.

Leo considered his drink options. Instinctively he thought to steer clear of alcohol. He had a job to do and needed to keep his wits about him. But he'd been working all day and had nothing to do now until the morning. What harm could it do? As he prepared to order from a passing waiter, Leo changed his mind again. He hadn't eaten much, and Kathmandu was at altitude. It was safer to stay off the beer for now.

Instead he ordered a bottle of water and began to flick through the menu. Many dishes were clearly named for the benefit of tourists: Sherpa Chicken, Gurkha Chulo, Everest Stew.

As Leo was trying and struggling to decode one of the menu's awkwardly translated descriptions, a beer appeared on the table. By the time Leo noticed, the waiter was already taking an order from the American couple nearby. Leo snagged up the bottle and changed his mind again. One wouldn't hurt.

He ordered a range of dishes. He knew it would be too much food, but it was cheap and he was hungry.

Far above the hanging lanterns, lightning rippled across the dusky strip of sky. Dampened by the layers of heavy clouds shrouding the city, it was far enough away to be over the mountains, but there was no doubt it would come. Leo sipped at the cold beer and wondered about the rain. It was raining in Brighton when he'd left, and now electricity in the air promised the same. Leo knew the story of God flooding the world in punishment. On an international scale that seemed impossible. On a personal level, he was less confident. Maybe Leo had upset the Almighty and was now his target the world over.

"Hey, you mind if we join you?" A female voice punctured his daydream. Leo looked up at the voice's owner. She was short and skinny, with aggressive red hair and an American accent.

"Sure, of course," Leo said before he knew what he was saying.

The newcomer waved her friends over. "I'm Jem, this is Katelyn, and this is Jack," the girl said, pointing out her friends as they crossed the restaurant. Leo introduced himself.

"Thanks for that, mate," said Jack, the last to sit down opposite Leo. "Really didn't fancy going back out on the street looking for somewhere else. Just need to eat!" He reached over and picked up the menu.

"You had lunch not that long ago," teased Jem, the American.

"Yeah, like two hours or something," Jack replied. "I'm a growing lad." He rubbed his stomach, then frowned as he tried to make sense of the menu.

"Have you been here before?" Leo asked.

"We've only just arrived," Jack said, looking at him over the top of the menu. "Came over on the bus from Pokhara today. An incredible journey, but so long."

"Yeah, I swear that driver was pissed," said Jem. "We were wobbling about all over the place."

"What's it like?" Leo asked. "In Pokhara, I mean."

"It's great," said Jack. "Very cool city. Lakes and mountains. Loads of places to eat and drink. What are you drinking here?" Jack picked up Leo's beer. "How is it?"

Jem and Kaitlyn were sat opposite each other and fell into conversation.

"Just ordered a beer," Leo said, omitting the fact he hadn't ordered it at all. "Wasn't sure what the local one was, but it seems alright."

"Yeah right, the local ones have been good so far. Gurkha's been the best I've had." Jack turned the bottle in his hands. "Ahh, Everest. This is decent too." Jack extended a broad arm in the air to catch the attention of a waiter. "Four of these," he shouted, holding up four fingers of one hand and Leo's beer in the other.

"Where had you been before Pokhara?" Leo asked.

"Two week trip from Delhi," Jack said. "All overland, a lot of buses and trains. But tonight, it ends." The waiter slid the beers onto the table. "Tomorrow we go our separate ways. Well, these two do. I'm around for a couple more days. How about you?"

"I'm..." Leo mumbled, not knowing what to say. He didn't know how to explain his job in Kathmandu without sounding like a fraud. He wasn't a detective. He was just a guy who knew a little bit about finding people because of some bad luck.

"Well, it's a bit of a long story..." Leo said, pausing, waiting for a distraction or a change of topic. Jack encouraged him with a flick of the bottle. Leo sighed. "I'm basically here to find a missing person."

Jack's eyes widened. "That's so cool," he said. "Who?"

Leo explained about Allissa, about Stockwell, about the website. Jack, Kaitlyn and Jem gasped at Stockwell's out-of-the-blue message, looked excited when Leo told them he'd accepted it, and smiled when he described his efforts in Kathmandu so far.

"How did you start out looking for missing people then?" asked Jem as Leo took a long, restorative sip of his beer.

Leo glanced at the people around the table. He'd known them for less than thirty minutes, but he was already opening up to them. At home, he didn't talk about Mya, the website or his hopes of finding her. People seemed to treat him differently once they found out. On the other side of the world, though, in the warm company of strangers, there seemed to be none of that judgement.

Drawing a deep breath, Leo began to explain.

32

"I've got it all planned," Mya says as Leo walks into the front room. The afternoon light pours through streaky windows and lies in angular patches on the floor. The sombre shriek of seagulls are still audible through the thin glass. "We need to go for two months though," she says, looking toward him, judging his reaction.

"I thought we said one month?"

"We did, at first, yeah, but then I looked at this." She indicates the map stretched out on the floor. "By the time we've paid for the flights, we might as well stay the extra month. Come here. I'll show you."

Leo's had a long, tiring week at the newspaper and wants nothing more than to sit still and close his eyes.

"It's literally the trip I've always wanted," Mya says, beckoning him across the room.

Leo smiles reluctantly and crosses the room. Mya begins to trace their proposed journey with a delicate finger.

"We'll go to Mumbai first," she says. "That's on the west coast of India. It's the capital city, although not the largest, but it'll be great to see — a real introduction into Asia. You can go and visit the real slums and everything, see the people who live there... "

Leo sits on the sofa and watches Mya. As she looks up at him, he nods. He wants to please her so much. He wants to. But he just can't. How can he tell her two months is impossible? Getting the editor to agree to one has been hard enough. The problem is, with the recent takeover of the paper, staff leaving, things changing, they can't do without him. The only way he's been able to get one month off is by promising to check-in online every couple of days, though he hasn't told Mya that yet.

But you deserve the time off, is what she'll say. *They don't care about you. They're wasting your time.*

And the hardest thing is, Leo partly agrees. Maybe he is wasting his time. But right now, he doesn't know what else to do. It's his job, the career he's chosen. Until something else comes along, that's what he has to do.

"Then for the second month," Mya continues, turning to look at him. Leo feels her smile thawing his frustration. "... we'll fly over to Bangkok..."

There's also the decision he's made. The biggest ever. A decision so big, he'll need a job to see it through. Weddings are expensive. But it's a decision he thinks, looking at Mya as she talks of adventures they'll share on mountains and beaches and islands, will be the best one of his life.

33

I n the restaurant with the Chinese lanterns, Jack, Jem and Kaitlyn listened in silence as Leo told of Mya's disappearance.

"I almost wasn't going to come," Leo said. "I don't know anything about finding people in the real world, but I thought, what would Mya want me to do? So, I came to look for this girl. Sounds pretty unbelievable, doesn't it?"

There followed three silent stares from the others around the table. It felt strange for Leo to be this honest with people he hardly knew. He was enjoying it.

"Wow, man, that's awesome," Jack finally said. "Some old millionaire has basically paid you to come on holiday to try and find his daughter?"

"Yeah, I guess. Though it's not really been a holiday so far," Leo added, straightening with pride.

"That's so sad about your girlfriend, though," said Jem. "That must've been awful."

"Yeah, it was." Leo nodded. "I've had no luck finding her. She's not been seen anywhere in two years."

"Man, that's so hard," said Kaitlyn, shaking her head. "I wouldn't even know where to start looking, nor what to do."

"Well, that's the thing," Leo said, "most people don't. There's no clear way even to start, particularly when it's in a different country and they're adults. That's why I set the site up."

The other three nodded.

"So, you're like some kind of detective now," Jack said.

"How are you going to find her?" Jem asked.

"I'd done a fair bit of research before leaving England. I started to trace her today. I know where she's been. Now I just need to work out where she is."

"What do you need to do next?" Jem asked.

"Bit of an obvious one. Find a local who speaks good English. Even finding a hotel around here is hard enough," Leo told them.

"Yeah, I can imagine... you'll definitely need that..." Jem said.

"Hold on a minute," said Kaitlyn. "What about Tau?"

The three looked at each other as though Kaitlyn's idea had entranced them all.

"Who's Tau?" asked Leo.

34

Two miles away across Kathmandu, Allissa, Chimini and Fuli rushed in and out of the guest-house's seven rooms. Together they made beds, folded towels, swept floors and busied themselves with the finishing touches.

By the time the work was complete and the three sat together around the small kitchen table, the night's darkness had long since descended.

To Allissa and Chimini, the guesthouse represented months of hard work. Months of calculating finances, finding the location, agreeing on a deal with the owner, and now setting up the rooms for the guests. To Fuli, it represented a future. A new start, from which she could build a life for herself.

"I bought something for us, for this night," Allissa said, standing and crossing to the fridge. The girls watched as she removed a bottle.

"What is it?" Chimini asked.

"Champagne," Allissa said. The girls looked at her blankly. "It's a fizzy wine we have in England when we're celebrating something. You do *not* want to know how much it cost."

"Fizzy wine?" Chimini repeated.

"You wait 'til you try some," Allissa said. "You'll love it."

Allissa placed the bottle in the middle of the table, then pulled three mugs of different colours and sizes from a cupboard. They definitely weren't the crystal flutes which adorned the tables of her teenage years, but they would do the job.

"This might make a bit of noise," Allissa said, removing the wire cage. Chimini warned Fuli, whose grin hadn't dropped all evening.

The girls looked excitedly from one to another as the cork popped in Allissa's steady hands, and a tiny stream of bubbles ran down the stem of the bottle.

"Now we have to do this." Allissa poured champagne into each of the cups and pushed them across the table. "Hold them up like this."

Allissa looked at the two young women. It was a moment she knew she wanted to remember. "To the future." Allissa's eyes moistened at their beaming smiles as she took her first sip.

35

Tau, as it turned out, wasn't local at all. He was from Varanasi in northern India. He had travelled with Jack, Jem and Kaitlyn, and now was staying on in Kathmandu to see friends. During the trip, he'd used a number of languages with local people and never failed to get what the group wanted. As the three described him, Leo saw an excitement come over them, like they were suddenly involved in the hunt themselves.

"Yeah, if anyone can sort something, it's Tau," Jack said.

"He knows all the parties." Jem grinned at a memory. "It was the end of the night. We thought things were winding down until he piled us all into the back of a tuk-tuk and sent us off to this bar. We were smashing it through the streets, no idea where we were going, but he found it for us. This guy knows all sorts."

"He sounds like a good person to know," Leo admitted.

"He'll know exactly what to do," Jack said. "He's been to Kathmandu loads of times, so he should be able to help you with everything."

An outgoing guy who knew the local area and who

could speak the language was exactly what Leo needed. Looking around at the others, Leo dared to let a feeling of positivity rise inside him.

"Where do we find this guy?" he asked.

"We're meeting him later tonight," Jack said. "He told us about a bar here, his favourite place in Kathmandu. These two are off tomorrow, so it's really our final night together. We're definitely going to celebrate that."

Jem was travelling on, down towards Southeast Asia. Kaitlyn was going home, back to Cambridge in England. She glowed when she mentioned her boyfriend collecting her from the airport. She made it sound like the trip away had been challenging.

Jack took a packet of cigarettes from his jeans and offered them around the table. Leo and Kaitlyn shook their heads, Jem took one.

"Let's get some food then," Jack said. "Then head over to this bar. It's the place to be in Kathmandu, apparently. Come with us Leo, we'll introduce you to Tau."

Leo had planned to go back to his hotel and get some rest ahead of a productive day tomorrow. Meeting Tau could be helpful. This could almost be a breakthrough.

"Yeah, you totally should," Jem said. "You'd enjoy meeting him, plus you never know what you might find. Imagine if we found her for you tonight. Like she was just there in the bar or something!" She laughed upwards, exhaling smoke.

"I'm not going to be out late though guys. I've got a long flight tomorrow," said Kaitlyn, looking over her shoulder at a passing waiter. Jem and Jack rolled their eyes.

More beers arrived, followed by the food; bowl upon bowl of creamy, luscious fresh curries, bowls of rice, and baskets of buttery naan bread.

"Most of the food here is vegetables apparently," Jack said. "Tau said there are loads of vegetarians because of their religions, but also because meat is really hard to get here."

He pushed a rolled-up flatbread into one of the bowls for the second time and scooped it into his mouth. Kaitlyn looked disapprovingly. Leo was getting the impression they didn't mind if she left early.

"I don't eat meat anyway," Kaitlyn said, carefully scooping one of the creamiest curries onto the rice.

"Ahh, you're missing out," Jack said, grinning. "The meat's been a bit shit on this holiday anyway. You see the scraggy little chickens kept in cages on the street. There's nothing to them. Not like the corn-fed fat ones we get at home."

"This is pretty good though," Jem said, finishing off one of the bowls. "Feels like we've not eaten in ages."

"You haven't. It's been like two hours," said Jack. "Mate, this girl can eat!" He flicked Jem a smile, and she kicked him under the table.

A group of young Nepalese men at the table behind Jack finished their colourful shakes and made off laughing into the night. The couple by the door ate slowly, deep in conversation. A large, plainly-dressed man sat in the far corner. He drank a beer and looked up from his phone to the restaurant and back again. He was at odds with the upbeat mood of the restaurant.

Watching the others demolish the food, Leo felt an unwelcome stampede of jealousy. It was as though they had a freedom he'd lost. Jem and Jack, it turned out, didn't know each other before this trip, but in the last two weeks had become very close. Leo knew how they'd feel when Jem had to leave in the morning.

When Leo and Mya were travelling, they'd stayed up late, got up early, and squeezed as much as possible into each and every day. Mya wanted to do everything, unless it was stupid and dangerous. Then she really wanted to do it. At the time, Leo often thought they were lucky to survive uninjured. Maybe if they'd been more careful things would have ended differently.

He knew he was going to have to do things that made him uncomfortable to find Allissa. Maybe things that were dangerous. And that started with meeting this guy, Tau, tonight.

Jack scraped the bowls with bread, then cleaned his fingers on a napkin.

"Right, let's go," he said.

"I'm going back to the hotel," Kaitlyn said, pausing Jack's rise from the chair. Jack and Jem made a convincing attempt to dissuade her, and Leo chipped in with some friendly encouragement. "It's been a long day, and that bus has pretty much done me in," Kaitlyn said, dismissing their efforts to change her mind.

"Let us walk you back," Jem said.

"No, honestly, I'll be fine. The hotel is only there. Thank you, though." Kaitlyn stood, gave some money to Jem for the food, and walked away.

36

Outside the restaurant with the Chinese lanterns, the restless Kathmandu night pushed on. The traffic had subsided to the occasional taxi, which stormed past in a hail of dust and grit.

Even in the day, Kathmandu wasn't easy to navigate. At night, when the only light seeped from windows and passing cars, it was virtually impossible. Each street wound organically from the next, as though it had grown that way over centuries. As Jack, Jem and Leo groped their way through the puddles of light and darkness. Leo reminded himself to make sure he left with the others.

After fifteen minutes they approached a man standing alone in the street. He was the first person they'd come across on the whole journey.

"That must be it," Jack said. "Just like Tau told us."

Jem agreed. Leo glanced up at the glowing windows which hovered against the sky.

"This is the sort of place you'd never find without Tau," Jack said. "He always knows where to go."

The solitary man opened a door between the locked shutters of two shops. The faint thud of music tumbled out.

"Tau says this place has been going for years." Jack's voice got louder to counter the music. "Torro's the guy who owns it."

Jack pushed open a second door and stepped inside. Leo winced at the smell of beer, cigarettes and the loud thump of rock music. People stood drinking and dancing around the small room.

"Tau!" Jack shouted. A man standing at the bar turned and beamed at them. "Tau, you gotta meet this guy we've met." Jack and Tau shook hands in an unusual way as Jack strained his voice against the loud music. "Tau, this is Leo. Leo needs your help. First we need beer!"

Tau offered Leo the same handshake, holding his arm vertically and cupping his fingers.

"Whatever I can do, man." Tau spoke the sort of English people learn by watching American gangster movies. "First though, beer! Yeah. You gotta meet Torro!"

Leo scanned the room as Tau led them toward the bar. It would be incredible just to see Allissa here. He looked around at the groups of people but couldn't see anyone who matched her description.

At the bar, Tau waved a note above his head as they shouted over the noise of the music.

"Man, that night was so good…"

Leo could only hear fragments of their conversations.

"I'm going to remember that forever…"

"Your face was incredible…"

Tau was acting out some part of the remembered night when the barman approached. He recognised Tau, offered a handshake, but didn't smile.

"Guys, this is Torro," Tau said, pulling Leo into their

circle. Torro shook hands with everyone as Tau ordered drinks in what Leo assumed was Nepalese. Torro was a big man, wide and tall. He had long hair and one half of his mouth slanted downwards, giving him a constant frown.

"Torro don't speak English," Tau explained. "He's lived in Kathmandu for over forty years. He's one of the originals. In the seventies, Kathmandu was one of the destinations for the Hippy Trail across Asia. Loads of people used to travel here and just get lost for weeks. That dope man! Torro's one of those, but just never left."

Torro returned with four beers in one hand and five shot glasses in the other. The beers were distributed as Torro poured out the shots.

"The first one to swallow pays," Tau said, pouring the shot into his mouth and washing it around his teeth. Torro did the same, his sharp eyes following the other three. Jack joined. Jem did hers. Leo was last.

The chemical taste of alcohol burned his mouth. Two seconds. Leo had never been a big drinker. He'd taken shots before but never particularly enjoyed them. Five seconds. Leo watched the others, copying their swilling of the rancid drink. Eight seconds. Nine seconds. The liquid tasted like acid. Ten seconds. Leo was still going. He looked across at Jack's grimace, Jem's upturned smile, Torro's cool, unblinking eyes. Fifteen seconds.

"Urrrrgggh!" Jack shouted, pouring beer into his mouth. Jem did the same.

"Ahhhh, man, drinks on you!" Tau said, slapping Jack on the back.

Leo hadn't lost. He was surprised. Impressed. Torro regarded him with cool, unsmiling eyes. Maybe he was impressed too.

Leo noticed the walls were covered with dozens of small,

yellowing photographs. Each was a tiny portrait; the type used for passports or visa applications. Leo turned around. The photos were everywhere, covering every available space. There must have been hundreds of them around the bar. Each faded square contained a moment of official servitude as the person's features lost all expression for the flash of the photo-booth. Maybe they were people who'd visited Kathmandu, come to the bar, and left their photo. Leo wondered whether these people ever thought about the photo of their younger self on the wall of Torro's bar in Kathmandu.

The next few hours ran like liquid from a glass. Beer after beer was poured. Shots were downed. Jack and Jem spent most of the time talking closely, leaving Leo to tell Tau about his search for Allissa.

"We can sort that," Tau said confidently. "What do you know about this chick, then?"

"There's something interesting about her family. She's got a half-brother and a sister. I believe she feels a bit like the odd one out. That may have something to do with this."

"Was she travelling alone?"

"As far as I know, yes. She left on her own, but she's been away for two years now, so she could be with anyone."

"Okay," Tau said decisively. "What's your feeling? Is she in the city or has she moved on?"

"I'm not sure, but I'm going to assume she's still here until I learn otherwise."

Tau paused as he ran through places in his mind. "That gives us a few options. Let's talk in more detail tomorrow and make a plan. Now we drink!" He banged on the bar and Torro lumbered over.

Around the room, sweaty bodies moved to the beat of the music. An hour ago, there had only been a few people in the room. Now it was difficult to move about. One song faded and the next began — *'London Calling',* by The Clash.

Leo looked around and realised he couldn't see Jack and Jem. While talking to Tau, he'd assumed they'd cornered themselves for a bit of privacy. Now, straining his eyes in the darkness, he couldn't see them at all. A lone man sat in the place where Jack and Jem and been. The man repeatedly looked down at his phone and up to the people in the busy bar. The light from the screen washed his face in an eerie blue glow.

Where were Jack and Jem? Leo was worried about getting back to the hotel without them. The city was a labyrinth of roads which all looked the same.

Tightness grew in his chest.

The music thumped.

Leo remembered how quickly Jack and Jem had forgotten about Kaitlyn — someone they'd spent weeks with.

Noise. Heat. His chest grew tighter.

Focus on breathing.

A cool hand touched his arm.

"You alright, lad?" Jack said, pushing his way through the crowd. "You looked like you were gonna go, then. It's a bit mad in here to be fair, eh!"

"Yeah, fine," Leo said, exhaling. "This stuff's potent." He held up the beer.

"Yeah, we're feeling the same. Just been outside to cool down for a bit. We're gonna shoot off now, Jem's last night an all. Do you wanna walk back with us or stay with this mad one?" Jack pointed at Tau, who was absorbed in conversation.

"Nah, I'll come with you."

Jack tapped Tau on the shoulder. "We're off mate. Jem's flying tomorrow."

"I'll come and say goodbye."

The air outside was cooler, though still not refreshing. The traffic had dwindled but the smell of choking exhaust still lingered.

Tau was first over to Jem. He hugged her and then disappeared back inside.

"Let's go," Jem said, taking a deep breath and turning to Jack. "We're on the clock tonight."

Jack put his arm on the base of Jem's back and kissed her on the neck.

Seeing their affection, Leo thought of the photos on the walls of the bar. Those photos were the faded ghosts of good times in the past. For Jack, that's what Jem would be tomorrow. Just a memory. Leo knew a thing or two about memories. He knew that, however much you wanted them to stay fresh in your mind, age would fade them. Just like the pictures on the wall of the bar.

That's the way memories worked. They were the past, and once something was in the past, you could never get it back, however much you wanted it.

37

The restaurant was busy. Travellers continued to find their way to the door identified only by the bare bulb.

Look for the light. You've got to look for the light.

It had never been advertised. The location wasn't officially known. Yet somehow, the legend of the Himalayan Lamb passed from tourist to tourist in the hostels and bars of the mountain city.

Over the years, the restaurant had received much critical acclaim, once making it into a guidebook. *"You have not been to Kathmandu unless you've eaten there,"* the listing said, giving vague directions about how to find it in the warren of criss-crossing passages. In truth, it would be impossible to find during the day, or when the bulb was not illuminated, which added to the elusive excitement travellers lapped up.

In the corner of the dark room sat a couple, their loud New York accents carrying on the spiced air. They hadn't noticed the waiter with the oily smile watching them from the darkness. They hadn't noticed him flick the switch on the wall. Turning the light off. Making the restaurant impossible to find. Nor would they notice his smile when, after the restaurant had emptied, he offered them the smoke.

38

When Marcus Green focused on a story, he thought of little else. People had compared his style of resilience and focus to that of a dog with a bone. When he was investigating something, he would continue until he found what he needed, regardless of what his investigation brought up. Since his meeting with his editor two days ago, Blake Stockwell was very much in the grip of his teeth.

The investigation had started on the expenses claimed by British members of parliament, but got interesting when Green started to dig into Stockwell. A career politician, Stockwell had been in government for longer than most, and as such, he commanded respect that frequently prevented criticism. To Green, this impenetrability just made the Lord all the more appealing. Stockwell had secrets, and the more Green dug into them, the more he got the feeling they weren't just embarrassing secrets, but criminal.

Green's interest intensified when he'd developed a suspicion that Stockwell was somehow mixed up in the robbery of a bank a few months ago. Of course, Green wasn't suggesting the ageing politician pulled on a balaclava and stormed in there himself. Maybe he wasn't even that closely involved, but he was somehow linked.

What Green needed was to talk to someone who knew Stockwell. Someone who could shed some light on what his life was like. Green needed a new angle for the enquiry, and he hoped the conversation he was about to have would provide it.

Green pulled up outside Richmond House, a twenty-storey concrete tower block in West London. He got out and, observing a group of hooded boys sitting on a wall across the street, double checked he'd locked the BMW.

Ann Bailey had worked with the Stockwells for twenty years. Speaking with Green on the phone the previous day, she said she knew many things that Green may find interesting. She added that she might be convinced to talk if the price was right.

Ignoring the entry system, which Ann said was broken, Green stepped into the dank stairwell. It would be an interesting conversation, he thought, as his footsteps echoed up the concrete stairs. He looked forward to getting to know the real Blake Stockwell.

39

Storms rolled around Kathmandu during the night, but none managed to break into the city. Sooner or later they would crack the anticipation which hung thick and heavy in the air. It left a bad taste in the mouth — electricity, dust and precipitation.

Leo lay awake in his hotel room, listening to thunder crash and tumble. He hoped no one would be hurt on the mountain passes as the storms pushed through the valleys.

After getting back from the bar, he'd showered, changed and gone to bed. He hadn't realised how much he'd drank until he lay down. The walls seemed to move and sway with his thoughts, and the rattle of the ceiling fan amplified to such a volume that he wondered how anyone in the building could ever sleep.

With growing frustration, Leo tried to work out what time it was in Brighton right now. But the concept of time and travel tied him in cognitive knots, and as usual, all he ended up thinking about was Mya.

He should have said, *"No, you can't always have it your way."*

She shouldn't have expected that of him. He was angry, sad and tired. At her, at himself, at being in this hotel on his own in a strange city, at Torro's unusual citrus shot that he could still taste on his breath, at the world for taking away things that were good and pure and honest, and at the fact that he hadn't had a proper night's sleep in nearly two days.

Finally, the tiredness took over and Leo succumbed to Kathmandu's disturbed sleep.

Leo awoke after what seemed like a heartbeat. Light piled in through the half-open curtains. His eyes adjusted as his brain registered confirmation on his location. He searched without movement for any injuries, and scanned the final memories of the night before. He wasn't used to drinking that much.

Confident that he'd remembered everything, sure he wasn't hurt, and certain he was in his hotel room, Leo finally sat up. In those first moments of wakefulness, he knew that people would believe anything. The disorientation that came after sleep was absolute and debilitating. He remembered one morning at university being woken by a house-mate saying it was seven am and that he was late for his part-time job. He didn't realise it was actually two am until he came downstairs in his work uniform to find the house-mate and five other friends waiting in fits of laughter.

Before leaving the bar last night, Leo and Tau swapped phone numbers. Leo had hoped they'd be able to get started that morning. Perhaps, with the way he felt now, it would be better to wait until the afternoon.

He reached for his phone on the bedside table. Two texts.

The first from Stockwell: *You're in Kathmandu now. I expect to hear news soon.*

The second from Tau: *Dude, I'll be at your hotel in thirty minutes.*

It was sent at twelve-thirty. Twenty minutes ago.

Leo sighed. How had Tau managed that? He was still going strong in the bar when Leo left last night. *Must be a machine.*

Fifteen minutes later, Leo scuttled down the stairs to the hotel lobby. He didn't want to keep Tau waiting; finding him was a step forward in the investigation, and he needed all the help he could get.

Tau rose from one of the bedraggled sofas on the far side of the gloomy space. He wore dark leather shoes, blue faded jeans and a baggy t-shirt with a logo Leo didn't recognize. His clothing and manner seemed to show an understanding of both the city they were in and the world Leo knew. Leo found it reassuring.

"How'd you like Torro's then?" Tau asked. He held his hand out for his trademark handshake. Leo took it, and let his breath go slowly as an answer.

"It was fine while I was there... when I got back here was the problem."

"Yeah, you look like you're in trouble, dude!" Tau said. "Let's get some coffee, then we'll make a plan. Have you brought the stuff you have on this girl?" Tau nodded toward Leo's empty hands.

A few minutes later Leo returned with the folder of information he had collected on Allissa and the Stockwell family. Tau was waiting by the door. Through the dirty glass, the world looked bright and chaotic. Leo followed Tau out into the chaos, and concentrated as they walked side by side in the gap between the buildings and the searing traffic. They had to avoid rubbish, abandoned vehicles and drainage ditches. Twice they dodged goats tied to the side of the buildings.

Tau chose a café, and they sat at a large wooden table at the window. The place was air-conditioned and quiet.

"I reckon you need to eat," Tau said, flicking Leo a menu.

Tau ordered eggs and Leo tried to explain to the waitress the phenomenon of cheese on toast. Tau was already coming into his own, offering some words of translation that the waitress hadn't understood. They both ordered large coffees. The caffeine would be necessary to get on with the day. Nepali coffee, Tau explained, was served dark and bitter, and without milk.

The coffee arrived quickly, followed minutes later by the food. Tau's eggs were the yellow colour eggs seemed to be in Asia and would without doubt be spicy. The sight made Leo even more hungry. This cheese on toast was going to be good. By the time the waitress put the plate down in front of Leo, he was so ready for it. Looking at the plate, his heart sank — two bits of cold toast and a block of cheese. Leo exhaled the disappointment. Today was going to be challenging, he could tell.

When the caffeine started to buzz, Leo and Tau turned to the business at hand.

"Show me what we've got," Tau said, rubbing his hands together. Leo opened the folder.

"Allissa Stockwell," Leo announced, producing the photo he thought would be her greatest likeness, the one from the beach.

"She's a pretty girl," Tau said, reaching out for the photo and examining it closely.

"She is," Leo agreed. "It was her father, Blake Stockwell, a politician, who asked me to find her." He passed over the photo of the Stockwell family. "She's Stockwell's daughter, but to a different mother, I think. There's nothing known about who her mother is, or at least if there is I can't find it. Allissa just seems to appear in the family when she's about five. She keeps a low profile generally, but was brought up in the same way as the others."

Tau placed the photo down in line with the other on the table.

"How old is she now?"

"Just turned twenty-eight a few weeks ago."

"What's her story then?"

Leo ran through what he knew about Allissa. "They were expecting her to follow her mother — her stepmother, I suppose — into law. Then one day she just goes. No word to the family or anything. Just disappears. A few weeks later she contacts them to say she's gone travelling. She's fine, doesn't know when she'll be back." Leo shivered as the air-conditioner's stream of cold air clipped the back of his neck.

"And she didn't come back?" Tau looked up from the photograph.

"They hadn't heard from her until a few weeks ago when she contacted her sister, Lucy. She asked Lucy to arrange the transfer of thirty-five-thousand dollars from a trust fund to an account she'd set up here." Leo paused to judge Tau's reaction at the amount of money. There was none. "Lucy said she'd do it, but she needed to know where Allissa was so that they could all stop worrying. They had a long phone conversation one evening, and Allissa said she was really happy."

"Did you speak to Lucy?" Tau asked.

"No, Stockwell told me this. He doesn't want anyone from the family to know he's sent me to look for her."

"That's a bit suspicious," Tau said. "How do we know she's in Kathmandu at all?"

"Stockwell got the account number that the money had been sent to. He's a well-connected guy and managed to trace it to a bank here. I went there yesterday and pretended to be her brother. They told me she had been there, and it was obvious when I showed them a picture. They wouldn't tell me the address she'd given. Even for fifty dollars."

Tau's eyebrows twisted in concern. Through the window, a bulging lorry pushed past, almost scraping the front of the buildings.

"I don't think she would've withdrawn that money and left the city," Leo said. "I think she had a plan to spend it on something local. We work out what that is, we find her."

"Yes, *we* will," Tau said with emphasis, focusing his stare on Leo. "You're definitely going to need my help on this, yes?" Leo nodded. "Well, this rich guy is obviously paying you for it, so I'll need a hundred dollars a day, plus you pay any expenses."

Leo wasn't going to argue. Finding Tau was a stroke of luck, and not one he was going to give up.

"Fine," he said, reaching across the table now strewn with papers and photos to shake Tau's hand.

"We need to go back to the bank," Tau said, his face opening into a smile. "If it's the sort of place I think it is, then I have an idea about how to get her address."

40

When Allissa emerged from her room in the morning, Fuli and Chimini were already behind the reception desk talking in animated excitement.

"Hello, welcome to the Teku Guesthouse," Chimini said.

"Hello, welcome Teku Guessouse," Fuli repeated back. They'd kept the same name for the guesthouse as the previous occupants. Although they had considered changing it, for a fresh start, they weren't sure what to change it to, and there was already a sign outside advertising it.

Fuli and Chimini smiled as Allissa walked towards them.

"You will never guess what has happened," Chimini said.

"Welcome, Teku, Guessouse," Fuli repeated quietly.

"We have our first guest," Chimini said before Allissa could answer. "She checked in about an hour ago."

"Wow, that's brilliant," Allissa said. "All checked in okay?"

"Yes, yes, of course," Chimini said, looking down at the large logbook now with one of the rows completed. "Paid upfront for three nights, double room."

Allissa smiled at Chimini's excitement. The thing they'd wanted and worked so hard for many months to achieve had at last come together. It was there. It had happened. Turning toward the kitchen, away from the women at the reception desk, Allissa let the smile drain from her face.

"Welcome," Fuli began again.

Allissa closed the door of the kitchen behind her. She didn't know why she couldn't be as happy about the opening of the guesthouse as Fuli and Chimini. She wanted to be. Wanted it so much. Allissa thought that getting the guesthouse together would give her a purpose, a place where she was needed and a sense of belonging. So far, it hadn't.

Although she now knew a few Nepalese words, she didn't speak the language, and the few streets she knew around the city didn't make it hers.

Allissa filled the kettle, clicked it on, and looked out into the thuggish morning. They were all alike — herself, Chimini, Fuli. They had all been through things which they carried around their necks — millstones against the world. Allissa had left England in an attempt to clear her mind of the things she knew, yet the memories had followed her here.

Allissa rubbed her eyes with the heels of her hands as the kettle growled to a boil. She knew she would have to face him one day. She would have to deal with the issues that she held so close, the issues which had inspired her to help some of the most vulnerable people in the world. Rinsing one of the cups they'd drank champagne from the previous night and spooning instant coffee into it, Allissa thought that often it was with the same strength that you ran and remembered. The harder you ran, the stronger you became, the more vivid the surging memories. Allissa knew that two years of running, covering thousands of miles, meant nothing when the millstone of her memories was with her the whole time.

41

On the short taxi ride to the bank, Tau explained his plan. Leo was not convinced it would work, but felt an obligation to agree. It was the only plan they had. As the taxi drew to a stop, Leo looked up at the looming concrete building which housed the bank. It was as gloomy as he remembered. Tau paid the driver with the money Leo had given him, and the pair stepped out into the road. Traffic sneered around them on the thin strip of tarmac.

"Give me two minutes," Tau said, striding into the traffic. Horns and shouts of protest echoed from swerving vehicles. "Two minutes, but no longer. Oh yeah, and wear this." Tau pulled a baseball cap from his pocket and tossed it to Leo.

Leo pulled the cap down low to shadow his face, then stepped backwards and ducked into the shadow of a doorway.

Tau climbed the stairs and stepped into the bank. The room was as Leo had described. He looked around while he waited for his eyes to adjust to the gloom. Yellowed posters advertising the bank's services covered the dirty, white-washed walls, and a constant stream of dust skipped across the floor. In one corner the lights of the freestanding ATM blinked. The bank teller sat behind the desk talking aggressively on the phone.

Tau walked up to the desk, pulled out the grimy plastic chair and sat down. The teller finished her call and looked at him. It was more of a glare.

"I need to withdraw from a Worldwide Union account," Tau said in Nepalese. He fixed his most charming smile.

The lady rose from her seat and collected a large pad from a filing cabinet behind her. It was the sort common in banks twenty years ago — pre-printed forms with carbon paper to copy in triplicate. Tau knew Kathmandu well enough not to be surprised these things still existed.

"Number,"— she pointed to a box on the form — "photo ID and local address. It takes twenty-four hours." Her tone was slow and practised. "How much?"

"Twenty-thousand dollars," Tau said, his smile unfaltering. "I bet that's the most you've had through here in a while."

"You would be surprised," she said flatly.

"Oh yeah?" Tau grinned, trying to warm her to his conversation. "What would someone be doing with more than that in this city?"

The lady shrugged and jabbed the pad with the pen.

"Fill in." She dropped the pen for Tau to use.

"I bet it was some old man who wanted to keep it under a mattress at home. I hope he doesn't get robbed."

Tau picked up the pen and started filling out the form. He paused before inventing a ten-digit number to make it appear like he'd thought about it.

The oscillating ceiling fan creaked on its circuit.

At that moment, as planned, Leo barged through the

doors of the bank. He pretended not to see Tau and the bank teller as he looked around for the ATM. He needed to make it seem like he hadn't been there before. Tau snuck a look over his shoulder. With Leo's hair beneath the cap and his efforts to look baffled by the place, they just might get away with this.

"ID?" the lady asked, watching Tau complete the last box. She had so far ignored Leo, who now stalked toward the ATM.

Leo slipped one of The Best Kathmandu Guest House's business cards into the cash machine's slot.

"CARD ERROR" flashed immediately on the screen.

"What the hell?" Leo said loudly, attracting the attention of both Tau and the bank teller. "What's it doing? You can't do this to me!"

Then, Leo started to hit the machine, whacking it on its sides and top. He even kicked it twice, each time making sure the strike sounded worse than it actually was.

The bank teller shot up. "Stop that! What doing? You break it!"

She rushed over to interpose herself between Leo and the innocent machine.

Tau only had a few moments. He flicked back through the pad and looked for Allissa's name.

He scanned the first sheet. No luck.

The second. Still nothing.

The lady was trying to calm Leo, who continued to shout at the inanimate ATM.

"It's got my card! Without that, I have nothing!" Leo slapped the top of the machine. Dust jumped from its metal surface.

On the third sheet, Tau saw what he was looking for.

Allissa Stockwell, written in large, curvaceous writing in blue ink.

36,588 USD.

Local address: Teku Guesthouse, Redcross Sedak, Kathmandu.

Tau closed the pad, got up, hurried down the steps and out into the street.

Leo allowed himself to be placated by the bank teller. But, before she could recognise him, he turned and grumbled outside.

A minute later, down the road and out of sight of the bank, Tau and Leo caught up with each other. Each wore a smug smile about what they had just done.

"Did you get it?" Leo was the first to speak. He knew the answer.

"Did I get what?" Tau asked, his grin wide.

"An address? Did you get anything?" Leo's smile dropped, suddenly anxious.

"Of course!" Tau said after a dramatic silence. "Let's go."

42

Green let the door of Richmond House slam shut behind him. He turned the collar of his coat up against the light rain which had just started, and paced back to his car. The hooded boys were now taking refuge in a filthy, dilapidated bus shelter.

Ann Bailey had talked. She knew a lot. Twenty years of watching, listening and being ignored came tumbling out in what seemed like a few short minutes.

Green sat in the driver's seat and dug out his phone. He had recorded the whole interview. He set it to upload to his cloud drive. This couldn't be lost.

He leant back into the seat and let his eyes lose focus. He had a lot to think about now, and a lot to do. *Blake Stockwell,* Green thought, *will have to answer my questions very soon.*

43

Allissa turned, looked at the Teku Guesthouse, and smiled. How ever she felt personally, she was doing well. Her life, her existence, was benefiting the people around her. That brought her a contentment all the money, clothes and make-up of her youth had failed to.

In the warm afternoon sun, the guesthouse looked especially appealing. Allissa remembered the first time she'd walked across the small square and looked up at its brightly painted red and yellow concrete. Their guesthouse was the most welcoming in the building; she hoped that fact alone would bring guests to their small reception desk.

Allissa turned and walked in the direction of the market. She was buying food for dinner while Fuli and Chimini looked after the guesthouse. They'd already checked in two more people that afternoon.

"I'M GOING FOR A SHOWER," Chimini said in their native tongue. The temperature of the guesthouse reception was stifling in the afternoon heat. "Come and get me if you need anything."

Fuli nodded.

"Will you be okay?" Chimini asked.

Although Fuli managed okay when the young man checked in earlier, Chimini noticed the room key was passed across with shaking fingers.

Fuli nodded again.

Chimini wasn't gone long before footsteps echoed up the stairs. Fuli's smile vanished as two men walked into the reception area. Chimini's words circled her mind — *not all men are bad.*

For a moment she was back there. The curtain, his voice, the smell of sour whiskey on his breath. She slammed the memories away and tried to force a smile.

The first of the men was a westerner, skinny, tall and pale. The second, Indian, his skin tone darker than hers from long days spent in the searing sun.

Chimini had been teaching Fuli the English phrases she would need to work behind the reception desk, and she hurriedly racked her brain for them. She could do this.

Not all men are bad.

The westerner was the first to speak. It was a phrase she didn't understand. The Indian's translation a few seconds later surprised her.

"I'm looking for my sister."

The white man showed her a picture on his phone and Fuli recognized it immediately. She tried to hide her surprise. Men looking for you couldn't be a good thing.

"Not here," Fuli replied in Nepalese. "Never seen her."

The men regarded her with a steady look.

"Has she been here?" the white man asked, the Indian man translating.

"Not here," Fuli said again. She looked down at the large check-in book spread open on the desk.

"When did she leave?" he asked, persistent. Fuli felt them looking at her.

"Not here," she said for the third time.

"I'll give you one hundred dollars," the man said, showing her two fifty dollar bills, "if you can tell me where my sister is."

Fuli had never seen dollars before, although she knew they were worth a lot in the city. Some of the men had used them. She'd seen them changing hands, but they had been quickly pushed into a pocket or a bag as she'd entered.

"Any information you can give me would be very helpful," the white man said, smiling and showing Fuli the photo again. "I really need to find her."

The white man picked up one of the guesthouse's business cards and scribbled a number down.

"Call me if you remember anything, and the one hundred dollars is yours."

He offered the card to Fuli, but she didn't take it. He put it down on the counter with the number facing her.

The pair turned and descended the stairs.

"Who was that?" Chimini asked as she opened the door from the bedroom. Her wet hair was wrapped in a towel.

"Someone looking for Allissa," Fuli said quietly, handing her the card. "Says he was her brother. I did not tell them anything."

"Well done," Chimini said, turning the card over in her hands. "People looking for you usually isn't a good thing."

44

"There's something she's not telling us," Leo said as their coffee arrived. They sat in a small café across the square from the guesthouse.

"We don't have to rush," Tau said. "We can always come back here tomorrow."

They'd made progress, and that was good. Leo wasn't ready to give up for the day.

"I feel like she knew more than she was telling," Leo said, looking back across the square. Compared to the rest of Kathmandu, punctuated continuously with horns and traffic, this area was quiet. Leo liked it.

"It might just have been the translation," Tau said.

"No, there was more to it than that. I'm sure. It was her look of surprise when I showed her the picture. Something to do with her age, too. I think a girl of that age is more likely to lie for Allissa." Leo chased the thought out loud.

"You're just seeing what you want to," Tau said. "She was a bit confused, surprised by your questions. If she does know anything, maybe she'll call."

"I wouldn't count on it. If she knows Allissa, they're

friends somehow, and I think women of that age stick together."

"Money can be tempting," Tau said.

"We offered one hundred dollars for information on someone who we know has thirty-five-thousand," Leo said, gazing out into the square. "I wouldn't count on it."

An hour later Leo and Tau walked into the restaurant with the Chinese lanterns. Jack sat drinking a beer at the same table as the previous night. There were two empty bottles beside him already.

Leo had to be persuaded to go to the restaurant at all tonight. He couldn't have a repeat of the previous night's shenanigans. If he had a beer at all, it would strictly be just the one.

"How ya holding up, soldier?" Tau asked, putting a hand on Jack's shoulder and sitting down.

Jack didn't answer straight away, and shoved the bottle to his lips.

"I'm alright," he responded after a long gulp, shrugging. "Just girls," he added with a sideways motion of the bottle.

"It's nice to have you back." Tau grinned. "I haven't spoken to you for about two weeks, since she got her claws into you."

Jack smiled vacantly. It was forced.

The events of the day bubbled through Leo's mind as Tau and Jack talked. Tourists from neighbouring hotels slowly filled the tables around them. Many wore colourful, baggy clothes which would seem inappropriate in their home countries. In Kathmandu they bordered on an expectation. Not beyond hope that circumstance would bring him and Allissa to the same place, Leo checked each table in turn. Maybe a fortuitous stroke of luck was all he could hope for. As his eyes drifted from one diner to the next, he thought about Mya. Where was she, and what was she doing now? With all his efforts to find her over the last couple of years resulting in nothing, Leo wondered whether one day, perhaps, she would just turn up. Maybe they would be in the same restaurant at the same time...

Leo watched as a man walked into the restaurant and settled at a table in the corner. There was something curious about him. Beneath the baggy, faded shirt, a large but toned body seemed to ripple. Unusual in someone travelling the world with little more than a backpack.

"Leo, Leo?" Tau said, holding out the bottle of beer.

"Yes? Sorry, thanks," Leo said, taking it and raising it in a toast.

As the three ordered another selection of the restaurant's creamy dishes, and Tau told Jack about their adventures of the day, Leo couldn't help but keep his eyes on the man in the corner. Something in Leo's consciousness rang with the image. It was as though their paths had crossed somewhere before. It was the sort of instinct Leo would normally put down as just a funny feeling. Right now, though, a funny feeling could be the break he needed. It could be the difference that found him what he was looking for, and finished the job. If he were an experienced investigator, with knowledge of dark and dangerous tactics, then he could ignore these things. He wasn't. He was running on instinct, relying on the help of strangers and, he hoped, a good dose of luck.

Leo took a sip of the beer as he watched the man. Maybe he was here last night. They had been here twice, so for someone else to do the same was not unexpected. That was probably it.

"Right guys, I'll see you tomorrow." Leo finished the beer and slid a few notes beneath the bottle. "See you at nine in the reception, Tau. Jack, see you tomorrow night. If we find Allissa, I'll have two beers to celebrate."

Leo crossed the restaurant, his mind on the events of the day and the sleep he desperately needed. The food and beer were weighing heavily. He just wanted to get back to his room and close his eyes. Leo stepped out into the electric night without looking back.

The man in the corner raised his phone toward Leo and took a photo.

45

"He said he was my brother and he was looking for me?" Allissa said to Fuli and Chimini as they prepared dinner. Chimini translated to Fuli, who thought for a couple of seconds before answering.

"Yes, he came in here, with a picture of you and asked if you had been here. He said he was your brother," Chimini added, toasting the spices in the pan. The small kitchen sang with their fragrance.

Allissa looked morosely towards the onions she was trying to cut as finely as Chimini required. She thought of her brother. The last thing she knew was that he was working as a trader in London. When she left, he hadn't tried to contact her, not even once. Her sister Lucy had a couple of times. But, with a pang of guilt, Allissa had ignored the messages, ultimately changing mobile phones and closing down her social media profiles. She felt bad about that; none of this was Lucy's fault, nor Archie's. Yet, of the two of them, he hadn't seemed to care at all.

"What did he look like?" Allissa asked again. "Could you describe him in more detail?"

"White, westerner, thick dark hair, looked like a tourist," Chimini translated.

It didn't really sound like Archie. His hair was light, like Lucy's. Allissa couldn't rule it out for sure, though. Why would someone pretend to be him? It didn't make sense. Allissa looked down at the business card with the number scrawled on it, her curiosity growing.

If it was her brother, then she needed to know why he'd come. If it wasn't, she wanted to understand why someone would pretend to be him. She'd been away for two years, and no one had come after her. Why would they want to now?

Deep in thought, Allissa didn't notice the sharp, stinging pain in her left hand until a spiral of blood appeared on the chopping board. She winced, dropped the knife and ran over to the sink. The stinging subsided as the juice from the onions washed away. Allissa inspected the tiny cut dramatically.

"Didn't they teach you how to chop onions in your expensive English schools?" Chimini said.

"Clearly not," Allissa said, a wry grin forming. "I'll write a strongly-worded letter about it."

Chimini instructed Fuli to wash and finish chopping the onion that Allissa had started, which she did with a speed Allissa couldn't fathom.

"I know what to do about these guys looking for me," Allissa said. "I think you should meet them again."

46

At the far end of the twisting labyrinth of passages, the brothers prepared food for the evening's service. They had learned the trade from their father years before. He'd taught them how to do it quickly and without a struggle. The drugs were a new — and genius — addition. Many people went missing throughout the world. Helping one or two along the way didn't make a difference to anyone.

Their father had opened the restaurant in the sixties after travelling to Nepal from Tamil Nadu. He loved the vibrancy of Kathmandu, and worked as a chef for many years before setting up a place of his own.

But there was one scourge on the city. The plague that made his pulse race and his ears thump. The city was awash with vagrants. These western travellers used and abused the place he loved and called home. They came to use drugs, eat the finest food and squander the precious resources that the people who carried Kathmandu on their bare shoulders should have enjoyed.

Worse still, no one was doing anything about it. Some

people even made a small profit from it, opening their houses to the tourists, or allowing them to eat in their restaurants.

Then he was offered a job, a job which changed the course of the restaurant forever.

The brothers talked casually as they prepared for their evening service. One mixed carefully blended spices in a large pestle and mortar; the other cut an onion, the short sharp knife moving quickly through the flesh.

Tonight, as ever, the restaurant would be busy.

47

"This will help us sleep," Mya says, crumbling a bud of dried cannabis over two papers, skilfully compensating for the rocking of the train.

They're travelling north from Mumbai to Delhi, nearly halfway through the nineteen-hour journey. The train moves slowly, rumbling its way through fields where people amble home after their day's work. Whisps of smoke curl upwards from houses of rusty corrugated metal.

First licking, then rolling the spliff tight, Mya tucks it behind her ear and jumps from the bunk in the second-class sleeping section. Leo follows her to the toilet cubicle at the end of the carriage. They pass families bedding down for the night, children in brightly-coloured pyjamas, and older people playing cards.

Cramming into the cubicle, they close the door and stand over the hole in the floor used as a toilet.

Mya lights up, and the spliff flares to life. She takes the first inhalation, holds it for a moment, and lets the thick smoke go. It dances across the inches that separate them before streaming through the small barred window.

A violent hand knocks at the door, followed by barked instructions in Hindi.

"They'll go away," Mya says, taking another pull.

The hand knocks again. The same barked instructions.

A key grates in the lock and the door opens.

The train guard stands there. Mya holds the spliff in her hand; there's no getting away with it.

"You cannot smoke in here," the guard says.

"Where can we smoke then?" Mya replies cheekily.

The guard beckons them to follow and pulls open the train's door. Fields sprawl toward the horizon and the sun makes its final descent. The guard points to the step on the outside of the train.

Mya sits down, and Leo follows. The guard pushes the door, almost closing it behind them.

The rails slide sedately below their hanging feet. The countryside tumbles downwards. Big leaved trees, red earthen paths, new shoots of crops above square-cut fields. The corrugated iron roofs and patches of water reflect the pink of the sinking sun — a patchwork of light and dark beneath the cloud-speckled sky.

Now would be a good time. An unforgettable time. We'll never be here again.

Leo looks at Mya, her face pink in the dying daylight. The ring's in his bag back at their bunks.

He could do it anyway. The moment's perfect.

Leo inhales; the wet air smells like vegetation.

"I love how you never know what's going to happen," Mya says, breaking the silence and handing Leo the spliff. "I always want to keep exploring."

Leo knows she's right; that's why this needs to be perfect. He's got one chance to get this right.

Mya shuffles closer as Leo takes a drag. The train

rumbles around another curve and leaves the moment
behind.

48

The night brought little rest for Leo. After two hours twisting and turning in the lumpy bed, he gave up trying to sleep and opened his eyes. So far, he couldn't normalise his body clock to the time difference, and the events of the day stormed through his mind.

First, Leo thought of the case. They had made progress and were closer than they had been that morning. That felt positive.

Allissa had been at the guesthouse, that much Leo knew. Now they needed to find out if the receptionist was lying, or if Allissa had moved on somewhere new.

Leo rubbed his stinging eyes. The city felt restless and tired too. Allissa was close. He knew it. Something in the way the guesthouse receptionist acted told Leo she was near.

Lightning shimmered in the sky. It was still a long way off, but getting closer all the time.

Leo thought of Jack. He knew how Jack felt tonight; lying alone in the bed he'd shared with Jem the night before. He'd likely not expected to meet anyone on holiday. Jem would have taken him by surprise, as would the feeling of loss when her taxi pulled away into the stream of traffic that afternoon.

Then, as usual, Leo thought of Mya. They'd not even gotten to say goodbye. It was a night that should have been perfect. The night he'd waited for. It hadn't ended in the confirmation of their love, but in her disappearance. Leo felt sorry for Jack, but in a strange way, he also felt jealous. Jack's memories right now would never be this fresh or clear again. Those perfect moments would now fade, distorting in the unstoppable march of time.

Then, in the final breaths of his wakefulness, Leo felt she was close. It may have been the lateness of the hour, his lack of rest, or confusion in the new place, but he felt strangely optimistic.

49

The night brought no rest for the city. The storm still tantalized, with far-off cracks of lightning rippling through layers of cloud.

Leo awoke after what felt like twenty minutes sleep. The sun filled his room with harsh light. He checked his phone. It was nearly eight am and his alarm was about to annoy him. He lay still, listening to the hum of the air conditioner and passing footsteps in the corridor.

When his eyes brought the world into focus, he saw he'd received two messages during the night. One was from his mum. The formal tone of her messages always amused him.

Dear Leo, I trust you're having a successful time in Kathmandu...

She and his dad were seeing his sister and nephew for the weekend. He would no doubt have had an obligatory invitation if he'd been in Brighton.

The second message was from Stockwell.

Leo, I hope you'll have news soon.

Leo read it, then dropped the phone to the bed. He knew

the job at hand and was working as quickly as possible. He didn't need the constant reminders.

Leo walked into the hotel reception ahead of the nine am arrangement and took a seat on one of the dusty sofas. The cheery receptionist insisted on holding conversation until Tau arrived.

If Tau had stayed out late last night, it didn't show. He waved at the receptionist with one hand while removing his sunglasses with the other.

"Alright boss," Tau said, crossing the room. "You feeling better after your early night?"

Leo greeted Tau with the awkward handshake.

"What's the plan for today?" Tau asked as they walked for the door.

"We'll go and ask around in some hotels, cafés and shops near the guesthouse," Leo said, shouting the second half of the sentence to compensate for the noise of the traffic. "We can't just sit about and wait."

"Coffee first though, mate," Tau said, pulling his sunglasses back over his eyes.

"Of course, if it helps with the hangover." Leo offered a smug grin.

A few minutes later, both cradling large coffees, Leo and Tau started the walk toward the Teku Guesthouse.

The morning passed quickly. The hotels, cafés, bars, guesthouses, hostels and shops were numerous, though none were informative.

"We only need one to have seen her," Leo said as they stepped back into the street from a tourist shop. Brass Buddhas shimmered in a diesel haze.

Tau knew many places by location, if not by their name, owner and family history. Those he didn't, they stumbled upon. A hidden guest house occupying a floor in a residential building. A man selling bottled drinks from a cart. A large woman in a crimson sari selling leather wristbands and bangles. Leo and Tau asked them all.

"She was selling hash, too," Tau said as they walked away from the woman in the crimson sari.

"How did you know?" Leo asked, turning to look at the woman, now talking with a pair of tourists.

"She's been around for years. She always stands right there."

"Don't the police do anything about it? Isn't it illegal?" Leo asked.

"Yeah sure, it's illegal. She's not doing any harm. Arrest her, and who's going to feed her family? Plus, she couldn't afford to get out. They might even be watching her now."

"What, watching and doing nothing?"

"Watching is not doing nothing." Tau laughed. "They'll be watching to see who she sells to. The buyers will have money, and the police like to see a few tourists in jail every now and then."

"Why would they want to arrest them? They're not really doing anything."

"Look at it this way," Tau said, turning to face Leo on the busy road. "The police have to arrest someone, as it shows they're actively doing something about it. They don't want to arrest her, though, because she has a family that needs looking after and the suppliers are hard to catch. The tourists just make easy pickings. In here," Tau said, pointing towards another café on the left. "Definitely time for a drink."

By the early afternoon, they'd had a conversation with every receptionist, shop owner, or street seller within a mile of the guesthouse. Showing each of them the photo, explaining they were looking for Leo's sister, and of course, offering money if Tau thought it would help.

"You have to be careful who you offer money to," Tau explained. "If it's someone I know, or my family knows, they might get offended."

So far, it had all amounted to nothing. Some said no swiftly. On more than one occasion they'd been shooed away with the palm of a hand. Others thought for some time, flicking through hotel record sheets or inviting Leo and Tau to consult CCTV systems. On those occasions, Tau intervened, saying that the hotelier or shop keeper should check and call if they found anything.

Leo was certain, though, as Tau approached the table with their coffees, that he'd seen enough shady hotel receptions, dusty vegetables, yellowed newspapers and eager grins at the mention of money for at least the rest of the day.

"Something will come up, don't worry," Tau said, in reassurance at Leo's obvious frustration.

"She could be pretty much anywhere," Leo grumbled. "Particularly if she doesn't want to be found. We'd have no chance."

"My mother used to say" – Tau became solemn — "that the world is too crazy, too busy. People want everything now, now, now." He mimicked his mother's voice. "She said that when you really want something, you need to sit and think about the best way to get it. Running around never solved anything."

"Maybe," Leo said, trying not to sound sceptical. "I'm just not sure that works with missing people. They don't seem to return of their own accord."

"Well, it works when you lose something. I remember once, my dad lost something. We were turning the place upside down to find it. People were running everywhere, and we didn't really have a big house. I remember my mum sat in a chair and watched for about an hour until we were all getting bored and frustrated. Then she got up, and went to a drawer that no one had checked. It was right there. I've no idea how she found it." Tau looked toward the window. "But since that day, I believe there's always some truth in sitting and thinking about a problem when you're out of ideas."

"Where do your parents live now?" Leo asked warmly.

Tau didn't have a chance to answer. Leo's phone began to ring on the table, a long Nepalese number flashing on the screen.

Leo passed it to Tau. Tau answered the call. The conversation moved quickly. Leo couldn't decide if it was good or bad. After less than a minute, Tau hung up.

"That was the girl we saw at the Teku Guesthouse yesterday," Tau said. "Says she knows where Allissa is."

151

50

Marcus Green sunk into the driver's seat and let his eyes lose focus. Rain smothered the window with the windscreen wipers off, turning the yellow sign of the fast-food restaurant into refractions of colour across the grey London sky. The Stockwell case represented a good few months' work, and Green knew he was close. He pinched the bridge of his nose and shut his eyes. This portion of an investigation was always stressful. He'd been sniffing around so long it made him uncomfortable. Normally, the quicker the investigation was, the better. The longer it went on, the more likely the person being investigated would find out, and well-connected people found injunctions easy to come by.

Injunctions weren't the only thing to worry about though. Green watched two men in his rearview mirror. Hooded against the rain, they stepped out of a Land Rover and rushed toward the restaurant.

Right now, Green knew he held the key. The information was in his possession. All he needed to do was work out how it all went together. He needed to put it in the right order.

He needed to find the link, the connection that made it sing. If he could do that, then things were going to be very awkward for a very powerful man.

Another car pulled into the car park; its lights dazzled Green momentarily.

Getting the case together now was vital. Not just for Green's career, which rode from one freelance job to the next, but to those people Stockwell had wronged. That was another problem with the investigation going on this long: Green was starting to care. He needed to stay focused on the job, work out what it all meant, how it all fitted together, and what Stockwell's position in it all was.

Green was startled by the ringing of his phone through the car's speakers. He flicked a switch on the steering wheel to answer.

"Green," the editor said as a greeting, "I know you're working on this at the moment, so I'll be brief. One of the lads has come up with something that might interest you." The editor paused to cough. Green envisaged him sitting in his luxurious office just a few miles away. "It seems Stockwell made a few visits out to Kenya in the late eighties and early nineties. At the time it was reported that this was to grow export links with the president, but there were rumours that it was something more suspicious."

The thing about a case like this, whatever it was, was that you never knew when it was going to come together. You didn't know whether you were five minutes or five months from the breakthrough.

Kenya? What would Stockwell be doing in Kenya? Green's mind ran as though under the buzz of a stimulant. His eyes suddenly focused.

"It wasn't a great time out there. Single-party government, violence on the streets, different ethnic groups marginalised... perhaps exactly the sort of thing Stockwell would like to see here." The editor chuckled, a deep barrel of a laugh.

Green didn't hear; he was rummaging through the papers amid cartons of takeaway food on the passenger seat. Finally he found the photograph of the Stockwell family.

"Anyway, we've got people on that, looking into what was going on out there."

Green stared at the photograph, then flipped it over and read the notes he'd scrawled on the back. *Arthur (Archie) born 1985, Lucy born 1987, Allissa born 1991.*

"You there, Green?" The impatient voice of the editor rang from the speakers.

"Yes, yes," Green said, flustered. "I'm sending you a picture now. I think I know what Stockwell was doing in Kenya."

51

Allissa, Fuli and Chimini were in position ahead of the arranged four pm arrival of the two men. Allissa hid behind one of the bedroom doors and peered out at Chimini and Fuli at the reception desk. Chimini and Fuli spoke about the programme on the small TV as though everything was normal. Allissa couldn't see the TV, but heard its indistinct chatter.

Four pm came and went in agonising seconds.

Chimini questioned whether it was a good idea to invite the men back into the guesthouse. Allissa thought it was unlikely they would give up, and Fuli didn't think they seemed dangerous. In fact, if anything, the description she'd given was complimentary. Even so, Chimini slid the sharpest kitchen knife they had beneath the checking-in book and Allissa leaned a large metal pole up against the wall beside her. It paid to be careful.

Allissa looked around the newly furnished room. Frustration welled up inside her. They'd achieved so much in the last few weeks, and cowering behind a bedroom door felt like a step in the wrong direction. She hadn't travelled halfway around the world to continue to run and hide.

She pulled the blinds aside and looked down out at the square. Shadows from the skeletal trees spread like fingers across the dusty slabs as the sun began its descent.

That, she supposed, was the nature of running. You didn't get to decide when you stopped.

Allissa looked through the window and saw a man walk into the square. The way he moved intrigued her. He scurried, and then disappeared out of sight, as though hiding from someone. There were plenty of strangely-behaving tourists in the city; he must be one of them. He could have been here for decades, or just returned to relive a lost youth. Allissa watched the man appear again and walk toward the guesthouse. He passed a recessed doorway, paused, then hurried out of sight again.

Footsteps echoed up the stairs behind her. Allissa crept back behind the door and peered out into the reception area. The girls were still behind the front desk. Everything looked normal. The footsteps drew close. Allissa pulled the door closed to ensure she was out of sight.

Inane chatter reverberated from the TV.

"Hey, how are you?" Allissa heard someone say. It was a male voice. English. Neither Chimini nor Fuli replied.

Allissa smiled — the girls were going to make them work for it.

"You have some information for us? About Allissa?" the man said again, slow and simple.

Allissa pushed the door open an inch and peered out. She held her breath and willed her heart to beat more quietly. Fuli and Chimini watched the TV. Two men approached the desk.

After a few seconds, as though waiting for a signal,

Chimini pressed a button, silencing the TV. Stirring up a dislike for men, Allissa supposed, would be easy for women like Fuli and Chimini.

"Why you want to see her?" Chimini asked.

"She is my sister."

"No, she is not," Chimini replied. "Her brother looks nothing like you."

The man shifted his weight from one foot to the other. Chimini's hand slid toward the check-in book.

Chimini had given away the fact she knew Allissa well enough to have talked to her since their last visit. That didn't mean she was still in Kathmandu. It was worth it to expose his lie.

Allissa's hand closed around the metal pole as she watched the scene unfold. Although she hoped she wouldn't have to use it, the feel of the cold metal brought reassurance.

The white man cleared his throat. The larger, Nepali or Indian-looking man — Allissa couldn't tell from behind — stepped backward to give his friend some space.

"You're right. I lied," the man at the front said. His voice was soft and slow, like a promise. "I'm looking for her because her family are very worried about her. They haven't heard from her for a long time. They just want to know if she's alright." He paused for a moment. Fuli looked toward Chimini.

"They haven't asked me to bring her home or anything," he reassured the women. "I'm just here to check that she's alright. Then I can let them know she's fine, and be out of your way."

Chimini didn't reply. In the momentary silence, Allissa thought the man had been described well. From the back, he was slight and pale, with big messy hair. He was clearly an inexperienced tourist.

"Why should I help you find her?" Chimini asked after the silence had passed its breaking point.

"You don't have to help me," he said. "You don't have to, but..." He paused, making a choice. "I'm someone who knows what it's like to lose someone. I know what the sleepless nights and unanswered questions do to a person." He paused again, inhaling, exhaling. "My girlfriend went missing two years ago, and I think about her every day. Every day I want to know where she is. So, I help other people whose loved ones are missing too."

Allissa watched through the gap in the door. She knew people looking for her wasn't a good thing. Yet, this man wasn't the thick-necked thug she expected her dad to use. Allissa had seen those types around the house when she was younger. She definitely wasn't expecting the soft words of the man who looked like he hadn't yet grown into his skin.

"When Allissa's father asked me to find his missing daughter," he continued, putting the palms of his hands on the top of the reception desk, "I felt like I had to help."

When Allissa's dad asked me to find his missing daughter...

The sentence bubbled in Allissa's ears. *His missing daughter.*

It rose like anger. A flame in a cave, invading the darkness.

His missing daughter.

How could she be his, after what he had done? He surrendered his claim to her when —

The words came out before she realised.

"My dad's screwing with you as well then..."

52

"The cheeky devil." The voice of the editor rang through the speakers of Green's car phone. Green was alert now. Any thought of the frustration and tiredness he'd felt before vanished with his realisation. "It wasn't what was he doing in Kenya, but who."

"Run me through the dates you know he was in Kenya. Let's work this out for sure," Green said. He had pen in hand, and a fresh page of his notebook ready.

The editor read them from a list and Green copied them down.

"That's got to be it," Green said. "His housekeeper told me Allissa didn't arrive at the family home until she was five. It was one of those things everyone knew, but no one talked about. They all assumed it was just a regular affair."

"They're all at it," the editor grumbled. "That sort of stuff doesn't even sell papers anymore."

"But that leaves us with three main questions," Green said, thinking out loud. "Who's Allissa's mother? Where is she? And what was in the bank that Stockwell was paying so much to keep secret?"

53

Leo wasn't used to success. He was used to failure, disappointment and apologies. On occasion he reached an *almost there*, but success was something he had very little experience of. He was so focused on how he was going to find Allissa, that he didn't actually know what he was going to do if, and when, he did. Talk to her, he supposed. Then, tell her dad she was all good, collect his money, and get the hell home.

The moment before hearing the voice, Leo's attention was fixed on the young ladies behind the reception desk. Their hazel eyes showed nothing but innocence, a profound childlike purity which Leo felt drew the honesty from him.

"My dad's screwing with you as well then."

The bottom fell from Leo's stomach, and a lump appeared in his throat as he heard the voice. It was one he didn't recognise, but instantly felt he knew.

Leo turned and stood face-to-face with the woman he'd been sent to find. Allissa Stockwell. Alive and well. Right here. In the flesh.

She was taller than Leo had imagined, yet it was unmistakably her. She had dark skin, darker than in the photos he'd seen, the result of months in a warm climate. Her hair was dark, contrasting a pair of bright, expressive eyes which now burned in anger.

"My dad's screwing you over too, is he?" Allissa repeated.

When Leo came to his senses, his jaw opened slightly. "I hope not," he replied, shaking himself back into focus. "He's already paid me to find you. So, I suppose if anyone was screwing anyone, I was him screwing him. Until just now."

"He'll have something prepared. You wait. When he's finished, you see how long it takes to drop you," Allissa said, her voice serrated.

"As I just said to your friends here," Leo said, indicating the receptionists, "I'm not here to force you to go home or to do anything. I just want to talk to you so I can let your father know you're alive and well."

"You can do that now. Here I am."

"I have a few things I'd like to ask you. If that's okay? Is there somewhere we could talk?"

"All the rooms here are full."

"We can go to the café across the road. Coffee? Something stronger?"

Allissa looked at the two women standing behind Leo.

"Yeah, alright," she said. "But not for long. We have customers."

"LET me start by telling you a little about me," Leo said as they sat opposite each other in the café. Tau had gone back to the hotel, his work complete.

"I heard you telling Chimini about your missing girlfriend. Is that true? Or was that a lie to get her to talk? Like saying you were my brother?"

"Totally true," Leo said. "We were travelling down through Thailand. We'd had an amazing few weeks, then one night she just disappeared. Left all her stuff, everything. I just came back to our room, and she was gone."

"Did you try to find her?"

"I spent a few days on the island, but there was no trace. No one would help me either. The police were useless — they tried to blame her disappearance on a guy who worked at the hotel. I couldn't get any proper answers. There are only a few ways off that island, so someone must have known something." Leo pulled himself back into the present. "I've spent the last two years looking for her online. I set up a website, Missing People International. That's how your dad found me, I think."

"You help a lot of people like this?"

"I help a lot of people through the website. I tell them where to go and who to contact, but I've never helped anyone like this before... or actually found them."

"So, why now?"

"I lost my job."

"What did you do?"

"I was a journalist at a local newspaper."

"How did you lose it?"

"The editor thought I recorded a court case, got the paper into loads of trouble. It wasn't me. It was another guy who worked there."

"Convenient, that is, isn't it?" Allissa said, folding her arms. She softened with the higher ground.

"What?"

"That you can do something my dad wants. Then you lose your job. Then he approaches you to help him."

Leo hadn't thought of it that way before.

"Why did you get blamed for filming the court case?" Allissa asked.

"I thought I was the only person with the social media passwords. Turns out another guy, Callum, had got them somehow and logged in on his phone."

Allissa looked beyond Leo and out into the square. Leo leaned forward.

"Callum," Allissa said thoughtfully. "My brother had a friend called Callum. Last I heard he was a journalist. Dad was using him for leaking all sorts of government info, mostly lies about his rivals. Callum was doing well out of it, though, because it sold papers. What was his second name?"

Leo had to think. The world of Brighton, the incessant rain, the newspaper... It all seemed a lifetime ago.

"Martins?"

"That was it, I'm sure!"

Leo looked at Allissa. For the second time a lump grew in his throat. His breathing quickened. He inhaled deeply to calm himself.

"Why would he send someone who'd never done this before?" Leo asked. "Better to send someone experienced. He could certainly afford to pay for it."

"Because he's afraid they'd do him over. They could learn why he wanted to find me so much, then blackmail him or something."

"Well, why wouldn't I do that?"

"Because you're an out-of-work journalist who's still bitter about the loss of an ex-girlfriend."

"What's he so scared about me knowing?"

Allissa looked at him, straight and hard. Her voice, angry and bitter. "What he did to my mum."

———

54

L ights in the windows surrounding the small square flickered on as afternoon dissolved to evening. Allissa gazed up at the guesthouse on the top floor of the building opposite, its bright colours smothered by the coming night.

She knew that she didn't have to tell Leo anything. There was no obligation. Yet he was a victim too, in a way.

"I found out two years ago, and haven't been back since," Allissa said. "I can't bear to see him. And he knows I'll tell anyone I want because she was my mum."

Leo said nothing.

"As you probably know, I grew up with my father, step-mum and half-brother and sister. To be honest, they're lovely. Lucy, Archie and me used to get on so well. It was clear I was different from them, we all knew it, but it wasn't a problem. No one was bothered. In many ways, I was very lucky. I went to great schools and had good friends. I'd never really wanted for anything." Allissa paused, finished her drink, then signalled for another. This time she asked for a beer.

"I knew Eveline wasn't my mother. They'd told me that from a very young age. I assumed, when I was old enough to understand, that dad had an affair with my mother. Then after my mum died, I came to live with them. That wasn't the whole story. I used to ask dad about my mum, and he used to tell me things. I realised that Eveline didn't like it, so I stopped. When dad and I were alone together, though, I'd ask. He'd only tell me little things, but to me, they were so important. All I really know about her is from those moments. She was from Kenya — they met while dad was over there. He went a few times with work and they struck up a relationship. He can be pretty charming by all accounts. He gave me a photo of her. She was beautiful. Tall and elegant, with an incredible smile. In one picture she's standing with other people; they must be my relatives, I just don't know who. He told me — and it's what I believed for so long — that she'd gone back to Kenya to see some family, and that while she was there she had an accident and died. That was a lie."

Beers arrived at the table, and Allissa took a long gulp. Her eyes began to sparkle. Leo leaned forward, listening.

"Then, one evening, things weren't going well at uni. I got in an argument with someone. I can't remember who now, but I went home. I just needed to get some space. I let myself into the house as I normally would. No one was home. Lucy and Archie were away too. After a while dad and Eveline came in and I went to surprise them. It sounds stupid now. I heard them talking from outside the kitchen door. Something in their voices made me stop and listen..."

———

"You're doing it again, aren't you?" Eveline says, her voice raspy, angry, violent.

Stockwell doesn't reply.

"You just can't help yourself, can you? I know you've been doing it, but why?"

Silence.

"Didn't you have enough of that last time?" Eveline continues. She's shouting, now.

"Well, I sorted it last time, didn't I?" Stockwell says finally, his voice a whisper.

"You sorted it? You sorted it? We've been stuck with the result of it every day. Everyone can see it. Everyone knows. What was I supposed to do? I couldn't even say she was mine. And now you're at it again."

"Don't say that about our daughter." Stockwell's voice rises.

"Your precious daughter! Does she know what you did to her mother, because you were so desperate to be a family? Does she? Let's see how much she loves her dad when she does. I'll call her right now." Eveline reaches for the phone on the kitchen counter. "I'll call her right now. Then we'll see how much she wants to be your daughter!"

"Give me the phone," Stockwell commands, taking a step towards his wife.

"No, we'll sort this out now."

Stockwell makes a grab for the phone. Eveline moves out of his way twice, but on the third time he overpowers her. He's twice her size. She loses balance and falls into a cabinet of painted china. The sound of breaking plates hangs in the air.

"She needs to know at what cost this family is built." Eveline's voice is venomous. "She needs to know how you waited for her mother to be out of the country, had one of your Home Office mates reject her visa renewal, and then had her held at the airport. Two days she waited at Heathrow. All she wanted was to see her daughter, but she couldn't even do that. You had them put her on the next plane back."

"You need to stop talking now." Stockwell's voice is a rumble.

"Then, as if that wasn't enough, you got the courts to take the poor baby from her relatives. Because you wanted that, too."

"Shut up. Just shut up!"

The sound of broken glass.

"And I'm just supposed to be okay with that? Just accept that?"

The sound of a fist.

A gasp.

Another fist.

A stifled scream.

A door slams.

———

LEO WATCHED Allissa wipe a napkin across her face. He felt as though he'd not taken a breath in minutes.

"The man's a monster," Allissa said. "Eveline was taken into the hospital that evening. They said it was a riding accident. They never knew I'd been back."

"And this is the guy I've been trying to help," Leo said. "I'd never have taken his money if I'd known."

"That's not all," Allissa said, their eyes meeting across the table. Jewels sparkled in her eyelashes. "After hearing that, I knew I had to try and find her. It had given me hope, such hope that she might still be alive. I knew that if she were in Kenya, I could find her. It took me a few days to find my auntie living in London. I'd stayed with her when I was little, until he took me. There were photos of me as a baby on their walls."

Allissa stifled a sob with a swig of beer.

"My auntie told me what happened. For five years my mum tried to get me back. She spent every penny she had on it, but nothing helped. Every application was rejected, and every time one of my relatives tried to get near me his security team were on hand. She knew I was there, and she couldn't get to me. After five years of trying, penniless, and without hope, she was killed in a protest. She wasn't even attending — wrong place, wrong time, my auntie told me all those years later. Because of that man. That fucking man."

Allissa's body shook with grief. She wrapped her arms across her chest and closed her eyes. Leo moved around the table and pulled her head towards him. He didn't know the girl, she didn't know him. But he was there. He was involved.

"Let's get out of here," Allissa said after the tears subsided. "I need a drink and a change of scene."

55

L eo and Allissa walked into the sepia glow of the restaurant with the Chinese lanterns. At the tables, drinkers and diners chatted noisily as relentless waiters replenished their food and drinks.

Leo led Allissa to the back of the restaurant where they'd sat the previous night. Allissa ordered two beers from a passing waiter.

"What brought you to Kathmandu?" Leo asked.

"I was travelling through, like most people," Allissa said. "I worked my way through India, making it up as I went along. The only thing I knew was that I didn't want to go home. I didn't really like Kathmandu at first. One afternoon I got talking to a group of people who were here working for a charity. That's when things changed." Allissa told Leo of her trip out to the remote villages of Nepal which spawned the idea of the guesthouse.

The beers arrived, and they both paused to drink.

"I like how you've used money your dad gave you to do something so good," Leo said. "There's an irony there."

"Yeah, he may be a monster, but he's a very rich monster.

He'd given me a trust fund which I knew was worth a lot of money. I used it to set up the guesthouse. The girls used to be victims. Now they're business people. The place has finally come together. The girls know what they're doing, and the first few guests have arrived. I'm not sure they even need me."

Allissa let the words settle.

"It's such a good thing," Leo said, catching Allissa's eye.

"Yeah, it's gone really well."

"Don't the police or authorities do anything for these girls?"

"Yes, well, they are getting better. They used to just ignore the problem. There's a massive stigma attached to prostitution in Nepalese society. They would brush it under the carpet, leaving the girls with nowhere to go. Although, in the last few months they've really started to crack down. A couple of men from the gangs got long prison sentences last year. Hopefully that's made an example to those still doing it."

Leo nodded.

"It's started to make a difference to the girls. That's the important thing. Just the idea that the authorities care about them. It's reduced their shame."

Leo looked across the restaurant beyond Allissa. The lanterns swung in the thick evening air. The thunder had stopped, but the pressure in the air prophesied its return. Maybe later the rain would finally make it to the city. Leo saw Jack walk in and waved him over. Jack looked confused at the presence of a woman in the chair opposite.

"This is Allissa," Leo said as Jack reached the table.

"Hey, you found her!" Jack slid into the seat next to Leo. "That wasn't too difficult, was it? Leo told us he was looking for you a couple of nights ago."

"I don't know what all the fuss was about," Leo said, smiling too and telling how he and Tau had found Allissa, leaving out the details of their conversations since.

"Good work," Jack said. "I knew you'd do it." He turned to Allissa. "Does it make you feel important to have people out looking for you?"

Allissa had no time to reply as an Australian voice punctured their conversation.

"Alright guys, mind if I join ya?"

56

"He'd always be having these meetings," came the voice of Ann Bailey, Stockwell's old housekeeper from Green's mobile phone. "They'd be shut up inside his office for hours. All sorts of important people would come and go, some of them with security guards and everything. When —"

The voice was interrupted mid-sentence by the phone ringing. Green grumbled. He didn't need disturbing tonight.

"Green," the editor said, without preamble. "Got something for you."

This relationship isn't right, Green thought. *I'm supposed to be the one feeding the newspaper information, not the other way around.*

"As you know I've put a team on this. I think it's going to blow up in a big way. It's a bugger we can't do a bit of phone tapping, as that would blow this thing right open. Bastards like Stockwell love it. Anyway, we're still good to do a bit of old-fashioned pursuit. We've had a couple of lads tailing him, and the arsehole's been stopping at a village phone box near where he lives. What does he think this is, the Cold

War? Well, there's no law about having a listen into that, not that I'm aware of anyway. It's basically public property. I've got a few calls you'd be interested in hearing. I'll send them over now. Call me back when you've listened."

Green powered on his laptop and checked his inbox. The e-mail was already there. He clicked on the attachment and a fuzzy recording played.

"I need you to do something," came a voice, echoing in what Green assumed was the phone box. It took a couple of seconds for Green to realise the voice belonged to Stockwell. "I'll arrange for her to be taken there, yes. You'll do everything else, yes?"

Then a pause.

"Yes, she's already in Kathmandu."

Green turned the volume up to the max, straining to hear the voice on the line through the hum.

"It'll be tonight or tomorrow, so you need to look out for her," Stockwell boomed from the laptop's speakers. "I need to know you'll do everything. There can't be any loose ends... Yes... A woman in her late twenties..." There was a pause while Stockwell listened. "Mixed race. I'm not sure who she'll be with, but I don't care about them. Do what you like... Right, sure."

It sounded as though Stockwell was writing something down.

"You'll get your money. Call me when it's done."

57

"I see you've got a spare seat." Leo, Jack and Allissa looked toward the owner of the Australian voice. "This place is pretty busy... mind if I join ya?"

"Yeah, no problem mate," said Jack, indicating the empty seat next to Allissa. Beers had arrived, and the three were going through them quickly.

"I'm Miles." The stranger offered a thick, tanned hand around the table.

"What're you doing in Kathmandu?" Jack asked after the introductions.

"Living the dream, mate." Miles laughed and ordered a beer from a passing waiter.

"What do you think of the place?" Jack asked.

"It's not as good as last time."

"When was that?"

"1978," Miles said. "I was twenty, younger than you guys are now I'd say. Living in South London at the time. Me and my brother bought a van. It already had about a hundred-thousand miles on it. Yellow, and rusty as hell. My brother knew a bit about engines, so he fixed it up nice. I painted it.

We got mattresses in the back, sleeping bags, and one morning we set off. We were on the ferry to Calais at eight forty-five."

Leo, Allissa and Jack listened. Miles pushed a curl of grey hair behind his ear.

"We didn't even know where we were going, but we set off. You can't do that anymore. Everyone knows where they're going now. Got these sat navs and that. We just knew we had to go east. Got a compass glued to the dash. So we kept going east. We'd often meet up with other people doing the same — you could see their bright vans. We'd take turns sleepin', stopped when we wanted."

Miles spoke while the others listened. Leo thought there might have been some opposition to him dominating the conversation, but there wasn't. Miles' beer arrived, and he drank a third of it straight away.

"Back in those days, it was full of hippies on the way east. We travelled down through Turkey into Iran. Didn't stay in Tehran long, just passed through. They didn't have alcohol. Then into Afghanistan, Pakistan, India. Then we chose to head north, and came here. It's such an incredible feeling to travel that far overland. You really get a true impression of how small the world is and how many different people live across it. We left a raining, grey London one day, and four months later rolled into Kathmandu in the same battered old Transit. I remember it like it was yesterday."

"How long did you stay?" Jack asked.

"Stayed here for a month. It was the sort of place you just couldn't leave. Then we went back to India. We'd planned to drive home, but by that point it wasn't looking too good in Iran or Afghanistan, so we bummed about for a few weeks. One morning we got a letter from our parents with two airline tickets. They'd never been that keen on us going. They'd seen Iran on the news and assumed the whole of Asia was like that. Using them felt a bit like selling out, having come all that way in the van. In the end, we turned up at Bombay airport on a Monday morning and landed back in London that evening. And the worst thing..."— Miles took a sip of the beer — "the worst thing is, I don't even have any pictures of it. I didn't have a camera back then. All I've got to remember it by is what's in here." He tapped the side of his grizzled head.

"I can imagine," Jack said. "How did you fit back into normal life after that?"

Miles laughed. "Yeah, that was hard. Had to get a job. My first real job. A year later, I was married and had a baby on the way. The eighties came, and the world felt different. It wasn't quite as fun anymore. We were lucky to do it when we did." Miles looked into the middle-distance, then continued to tell the younger travellers about his three children, how they'd moved to Australia when his oldest was eight, and how he now had a collection of grandchildren.

"Your wife didn't fancy coming with you?" Jack asked.

"She died last year," Miles said, regaining focus on the table. "It was a total shock. One day she was complaining of a headache, which was totally unlike her. She took a few painkillers and went to bed. She just didn't wake up again. She'd had a stroke during the night. After a while, we knew she wasn't coming back."

The lanterns around the bar shivered. The night had taken on a chill. Leo drained his beer and added it to the pile of empties.

Leo looked at Miles and felt a sting of apprehension. Maybe it was just the conversations of conspiracy he and Allissa had shared earlier in the evening.

What interested Leo about Miles' stories, though, was how at peace with it he seemed. It was as though it had happened to someone else.

"You know, I always said I'd come back here," Miles continued, looking around. "My wife said she'd come with me. That's one of the reasons I had to come back. She'd heard so many stories and wanted to see the places for herself. We kept saying we would —"

"Well, you're here now mate," said Jack, "and it's good to have met you."

Leo looked at Allissa. She seemed content. Maybe the company was the distraction she needed. Allissa caught Leo's eye and he looked away awkwardly.

"You know all the cool places to go around here, then?" Jack asked. "We've only been here a couple of days," pointing at himself and Leo.

"I'm sure it was different in those days," Allissa said.

"Oh yeah," said Miles, his expression brightening. "When we were here before there was the most incredible restaurant. We went as often as we could. I've eaten at restaurants all around the world, and I don't think I've ever had a meal as good as at this place."

"What was it called?" asked Allissa.

"You know what, I've no idea. I'm not even sure it had a name. But I don't think it was far from here."

Miles looked left and right as new beers arrived, and the stash of empties were collected.

"You reckon you could find it?" Jack asked.

Miles thought for a while and asked a couple of questions about landmarks and street names.

"Yeah, sure," he said after a moment, smiling. "Of course I could."

"Well then... we're going," Jack said.

58

"What did you make of that, then?" the editor asked, answering Green's call on the first ring.

"Allissa, he's got to be talking about Allissa. She must be in Kathmandu."

"Yeah. It doesn't sound like the sort of plan a normal father would be making for his daughter, though, does it?"

"She knows something, something he really doesn't want to come out."

"That girl is the key to this," the editor said. "Green, listen. I'm raiding the budget. Get out to Kathmandu and find that girl, find out what she knows. Tell her she might need to testify too. I've got a feeling this will go to court once the CPS get hold of it."

Green nodded and tapped his laptop to life.

"I just hope I can get there in time."

59

O ut in the orange-tinged street, it was clear the group had already sunk a few beers. Their voices got louder as they walked. The evening pushed on, and the traffic dwindled to a trickle of cars, bikes and taxis. Of course, hungry cows still roamed freely.

Jack and Miles walked in front, laughing at each other's tales of travelling in obscurity and swigging beers they'd bought "for the road". Although Miles was taller than Jack, he walked with a slight stoop. With Jack's upright and boyish posture, they were almost the same height walking side-by-side.

Leo and Allissa followed the rocking pair.

"You don't mind coming, do you?" Leo asked.

"Seriously, if I didn't want to be here, I'd already be gone. I'll come for a bit of food then head back. The girls will be alright on their own for the evening. Plus, these guys are entertaining." Allissa pointed to Jack and Miles waiting beneath a rare working streetlight.

Miles dug out a pouch of tobacco and began to roll a cigarette. With great dexterity he dug out a bud of cannabis, broke it across the tobacco and then rolled it tight. He put it to his lips, lit up, and took a deep drag. The end sparked angry and red.

"You know what I'd like to see," Jack said, his expression turning sombre as he accepted the spliff from Miles.

"I bet you just want to keep on travelling," Allissa said, as she and Leo joined them in the island of light.

"I want everyone"— Jack paused to exhale — "to be able to experience what I have in the last two weeks. If everyone in the world did a bit more of this" — he waved the spliff around — "then the world would be a much nicer place. Much more... tolerant."

Allissa stood between Leo and Jack in the milky half-light. She agreed with Jack. For the majority of her life, she'd been surrounded by excess, intolerance and greed, but it had taken her coming to places like Kathmandu to realise it. It wasn't that she grew up around bad people; just the system they were born into told them that was normal. Many of them had travelled widely and lavishly. Allissa knew that it was one thing to look at the world from behind the glass of air-conditioned judgement, quite another to walk the streets, meet the locals, learn their suffering and suffer with them.

Standing beneath the streetlight, surrounded by people she'd only just met, Allissa remembered something Chimini had said to her at the first village they'd visited. The sight of the abject poverty had shocked her, but so had the happiness of the villagers. "We're all suffering somehow," Chimini said as they walked back to the car. "The only difference is choosing what to do about it."

"That's the shame, isn't it?" Jack said. "The people who could really benefit from this would never do it."

"I know it's around here somewhere, I remember this

street. I'm sure of it," Miles said. "It was a long time ago, but I knew I'd be coming back. I told Anna about it many times."

Miles walked on and turned into a passage that was even darker and thinner than before. The passage was so narrow that a car would struggle to fit down it, especially with the dark mounds of piled boxes and rubbish either side. The only light seeped from the windows high above.

"Do you know where you're going?" Jack shouted towards Miles.

"Nope!" came the reply from somewhere up ahead.

Jack laughed.

"We gotta look for a light," Miles said. "It used to be exactly the same as this, I think. There always used to be a light hanging above the door. That's how we knew where it was."

"We look a bit lost to me," Leo said from another part of the darkness.

"Do you know the greatest thing I've ever heard?" Jack said, his words starting to slur. "It was the Dalai Lama talking to some journalist in a suit. The journalist asked him about the meaning of life. He thought for a few seconds, then said that he didn't know." Jack laughed dryly. "If the wisest dude in the world says it's okay not to know the answer sometimes, then that's alright for me."

Allissa, standing behind the others, knew that although Jack's words sounded drunken, there was some truth in them. Having spent years of her life being told what she should do, where she should go and who she should spend time with, it was exhilarating to be able to stand back, sniff the air, and let the future come.

"You've got to look for the light," Miles said again, stumbling blindly.

Leo was beginning to think this was a bad idea. Each turn had taken them down a narrower passage, until they were walking single file through the darkness, following a man who'd not been in Kathmandu for forty years. Above them, the tops of the buildings were almost indistinguishable from the orange glow of the sky.

"There it is! I've found it!" Leo heard from somewhere up ahead. "I knew I'd still know the way. Forty years I've been planning to come back here!"

Leo could just about make out Miles standing at a cross-roads and pointing to the left. Leo and Allissa caught up with him and peered into the darkness. Concrete structures towered on all sides. Then Leo saw the light. Above a dark doorway, a bare bulb hung on a flimsy wire — the final fruit on a dying vine. Miles strode toward it without a word.

Leo glanced at Allissa and Jack. As Miles neared the door, it swung open. Without a backward look, Miles ducked and disappeared inside. Leo, Jack and Allissa exchanged glances. Excitement reflected in their eyes.

Jack rushed forward and vanished beneath the bulb too.

"What do you think?" Leo asked Allissa.

"We've come this far." Allissa looked around, then started toward the door. "We might as well go and see what all the fuss is about."

Leo hurried after her, and together they approached the bulb.

Leo swallowed. His throat was dry from the dusty night.

Allissa ducked into the gloom of the restaurant with Leo close behind.

"I told you I'd find it," Miles said as they were shown to a table by a waiter.

"We never doubted ya," said Jack. "Been looking forward to this."

A waiter arranged cutlery as they sat.

"I was here in 1978!" Miles said.

The waiter nodded nonchalantly.

Leo slumped into the small chair and looked around. The restaurant had less than ten tables, each one lit by a single hanging bulb. The tables were close enough together that the waiters had to be careful when walking between them. Most of the tables were full. Surprising, considering how difficult it had been to find the place. It was as Leo remembered Mya saying — *the more difficult it is to get somewhere, the better it is when you do.*

"We need to have the Himalayan Lamb," Miles said. "It's amazing. It comes from the mountains where the air is fresh and the grass is clean. It's really difficult to get, but somehow this restaurant does it. That's what we always used to have."

The waiter arrived with bottles of beer and Miles made the order.

"How you feeling about Jem today?" Leo asked Jack as he shuffled to find comfort in the low seat.

"Yeah, alright. Sad to see her go, but I'll see her in a few weeks."

"What's that?" Miles asked.

"Jack's had a bit of a holiday romance, haven't you mate?"

"Well, we just spent a bit of time together," Jack said, reddening.

"Tell us about her..." Allissa said.

Leo grinned at Jack's discomfort.

"Yeah, she's a decent girl."

"Details," Allissa prompted.

"We met in Varanasi and travelled together for a couple of weeks. You know when something just feels easy, like it's meant to be? It's been great. Totally didn't expect that to happen."

"Apparently they've not been without each other," Leo said.

"Nice one, mate," Miles said. "You gonna see her again?"

"We're going to try. She went to Thailand yesterday for another six weeks, but she lives in Canada, and I live in England. We'll see."

"How do you feel about that?" Leo asked.

"I'm just happy it happened." His voice took on a softer tone. "Right now, I'd love to see her again, but time will tell."

The lamb arrived ten minutes later. It thudded to the table in a thick metal dish. To Leo, hungry from the day's exertions, it looked incredible. The dish was full of meat, some on the bone, some not. It hissed and spat as it cooled. The four diners shared glances of excitement.

Miles was the first in, abandoning cutlery and diving in with fingers and thumbs. Jack was next, going for a large bone that rose from the top of the dish. He picked it up and gnawed the supple lamb, pausing every few bites for a swig of beer. Leo and Allissa followed with fingers, thumbs and teeth.

The restaurant, which had been busy when they'd arrived, was getting quieter. A handful of customers remained, some eating, others now slouched in their chairs.

"Man, this is taking me back!" Miles said, pausing mid-bite, a piece of lamb held by its unusually long bone in his clenched paw. "This is exactly how it was all those years ago. It's mad to think the last time I tasted this lamb I was twenty! All the things that have happened since. It's amazing the way life works sometimes."

Leo removed the last piece of lamb with his fork and examined the dish it was served on. It was long and thin, curved at the edges and rounded to a point at each end. Leo lifted it briefly from the table. It was heavy. Whatever dark metal it was made from was solid.

"That was really good," Jack said, leaning back to rest his stomach. Miles adopted the same slumped position. Allissa skewered the remaining onions with her fork.

"Yeah, decent," Miles said, as a lull settled over the table.

On the other side of the restaurant, two men climbed to their feet. One stretched and scratched his hanging stomach while the other dropped a few colourful notes to the table. They walked to the door and out into the night.

"I told ya it was amazing," Miles said, throwing his left arm backwards. "You guys had almost lost faith, yet here we are."

The waiter came to clear the table. He carried the dishes two at a time. *Probably owing to their weight,* Leo thought. Jack ordered more beers.

As one of the waiters lumbered off through the darkness carrying the dishes, another approached. His smile was a radiating half-disc in the glow from the hanging bulbs.

"Excuse me," he said. "As you are special customers, we would like to offer you smoke as our gift. Would you like?"

60

The night brought no sleep for Marcus Green. After his call with the editor, he'd managed to book an early flight next morning to Dubai, where he'd connect to Mumbai, and then on to Kathmandu. The journey was frustratingly long, particularly as he knew Stockwell's words would constantly roll through his mind: *"No loose ends."*

Green had run investigations on killers before, many of whom he'd brought to justice. He always found something animalistic about them, primal even. He was always shocked by the way they went against the very fabric of society by taking another person's life. But instructing someone else to end a life in the calm and business-like way Stockwell did it — that was something else entirely. Especially if, as Green assumed, that person was Stockwell's daughter.

Green found the thought disgusting, enraging and, strangely, inspiring. There were some people who needed to be brought to justice.

Stockwell was one of them.

61

"Yes, we do," Miles declared. "You guys haven't experienced the best part of this place yet."

The restaurant was almost empty now. The only other customers were a pair of tourists sorting unfamiliar bundles of money at the table by the door.

"I remember last time," Miles continued. "We spent the whole afternoon eating, drinking and smoking in this place. We came in about midday, and it was after midnight before we left."

The others said nothing. Leo took a sip of the beer. It was cool and tasted especially good with the latent, lingering spice of the lamb.

"You know something I've realised," Jack said.

"What?" Leo said.

"Loads of things in life are bullshit."

"What do you mean?" Leo asked, laughing.

"I mean that loads of the things we work for are crap. This is total freedom we're feeling now. It's what Miles had in his twenties before mortgages, hire purchase and package holidays. Yes, you might have a great house and a fast car, but is it worth giving your life up for? All you really need is a place to sleep, something to eat and clothes to wear, that's it. Why do you need that new car or the big TV when you're missing the opportunities to come to cool places and do cool things?"

Leo noticed Miles grinning. There was something in Miles' smile that made him feel uncomfortable. A mask had lifted from his expression and what Leo saw now was eerie and malevolent. Leo looked at Allissa. There was nothing in her expression that showed what she was thinking.

The waiter stood a large shisha pipe on the floor next to the table. It was almost as tall as the sitting diners. He lit the coals and then drew on one of the hoses. The coals glowed like the red eyes of a devil. He pulled on the pipe again and the shisha bubbled. The third time he exhaled thick white smoke. The waiter gave each of the diners a hose, stood back up, and returned to the kitchen.

"Nah, I totally get that," Miles said, half-focused and breathing out a lungful of the smoke.

"It's like these people"— Jack paused to inhale — "who're obsessed with taking pictures of themselves in front of everything. Some people we travelled with seemed to just be there for the monument selfie. They weren't bothered about getting to know the people or the culture. They were trying to own the world, not just be part of it."

"Yeah, you can never own the world," Miles said, stumbling over the words. "You can only be shaped by it."

"Guys, this is top," Jack said to Leo and Allissa, who hadn't touched their hoses. "You need to try it."

"Yeah, come on, man," Miles said. "You're in Kathmandu. This is what the place is all about.".

Leo looked at the hose. He felt hazy enough from the

beer and the smoke in the air. This was uncomfortable, foreign and dangerous. Allissa didn't seem keen either.

"I remember this guy we met in India," Jack said. "He was telling us about where he'd been before... Laos, or somewhere like that. Anyway, he'd travelled for days to see this big old waterfall. It did look pretty special to be fair. He showed us the pictures. I asked him what the water was like. He said he didn't like swimming. What a dick! You can't travel for days to see a waterfall and not go in the water, that's just not how it happens! Sometimes, whether you like swimming or not, you've got to jump in the water, because you might not ever go back there again."

Jack was right, Leo knew it, and he knew that's exactly what Mya would say too.

With her voice echoing in his mind, Leo picked up the hose and drew cautiously on the sweet-smelling smoke. Allissa did the same.

"Yeah man, jump in," Miles said. "The water's good!"

Leo drew on the tube, the angry red eyes of coal sparked, and the smoke filled his lungs. He would just have a little. A taste.

A warm rush covered him, like a wave from a tropical ocean.

Breathe in, hold, and out. The wave retreated and left the room further away than it had been before — a warmth remained.

"Mate, you're not wrong about this," Leo managed. "That taste, lemon, the spices, cool, what is that?"

"They flavour the water, put loads of stuff in to make it taste good, and cool the smoke," Jack said.

The wave came again. *Breathe in, hold, taste the lemon and the spices.* Leo held it until it was about to burn, then let it out. The smoke washed away every emotion, leaving a calm, blank beach. A desert island.

On the third wave, the room began to wobble. Distances changed, and noises became further away. The wave came and broke over Leo, the restaurant, Jack, Miles and Allissa.

The reason he was here, his success — Allissa.

Jack and Miles had been smoking for longer than Leo and Allissa, but Leo felt it affecting him already. The first three drags had hit him so hard that he'd stopped pulling on the hose. He needed to keep his head in the game.

The eyes of coal burned ferociously.

Talking was done now. The world shrank to the smoke and the burning eyes of coal.

Leo just needed to stay in the game.

Don't close your eyes.

Don't close your eyes. Focus on breathing.

Focus on breathing.

62

"It's just like drinking, isn't it?" It's not really a question. Mya's daring Leo to disagree.

"What's that?"

"Being with someone. It's like drinking,"

"What, because you keep going until you're sick?"

"No!"

They're in bed on their first afternoon in Goa.

"It's like drinking, because when you start, it's great, heady, exciting. You can't get enough of it. You just want more and more. Then, after a while, you realise you're not seeing your friends as much, and it's become more important than them. Then you realise you're not spending the time you used to with your family, and it's more important than them, too. Then you realise you haven't thought about anyone or anything else for ages. It's just you and the drink, or you and that person."

She tilts the bottle and looks myopically through it.

"We'd better get rid of this then," Leo says, taking the bottle from her and pushing her on to her side.

Her thoughts absorb him completely. They speak to his

understanding in ways he's never experienced before. He pulls her in close so that all he can see is her lips in the darkness. All he can hear is her breathing joining his. He kisses her from his soul, and their breaths dance in silent noise.

Two breaths in the silence.

ONE BREATH IN THE SILENCE.

Breathe in, and out. Breathe in, and out.

Leo floated above the chair. He held on for everything he could.

Breathe in, and out.

The room spun and swayed across his vision.

He'd only had a couple of pulls on the smoke. It was strong.

He tried to look at Jack and Miles across the table. They appeared as though in a dream, far away and moving further all the time. Leo knew that if he tried he could reach out and touch them.

He turned and saw Allissa struggling with the effects too. She stared into nothing, her jaw tensed and eyes wide.

No one was smoking anymore. The shisha hoses lay in their laps.

Miles' head was slouched forward. Jack's was back. The more Leo tried to reach forward, to tap one of Jack's arms which lay limp on the table, the further he moved away. Jack was at the end of a tunnel. Everything else was darkness.

Time curved in on itself as Leo's movements slowed.

He needed to stay focused, or he knew he'd fall...

Breathe in, and out.

Breathe in, and out.

He needed to stay focused, or he knew he'd fall...

He needed to fight this.

Breathe in, and out. Breathe in, and out.

Every molecule of Leo's body wanted him to close his eyes and relax. Each individual atom told him to sleep. The space between atoms, the vibrations of energy between the subatomic particles which made up his body and all of time and space, told him to close his eyes and sleep.

But he needed to stay focused.

He had to focus on the slumped figures of Jack and Miles.

He hoped Allissa was doing the same. Right now, he couldn't see her.

Then, through the fish-eyed tunnel vision which strained his brain, he noticed something. One of the waiters approached the table. Without a word, he removed the coals and carried the shisha pipe back into the kitchen.

A moment passed — a sluggish, immeasurable, treacle-like moment.

The waiters appeared either side of Miles. With a hand under each of his heavy arms, they raised him from the chair. His slumped figure gave no resistance as they lifted and then dragged him towards the kitchen door. His limp feet trailed across the uneven ground.

Leo watched them disappear in a haze. He couldn't do anything. He tried to move, tried to stand, but the room was spinning. His legs were no longer beneath him.

Just concentrate on your breathing, he thought. *Don't close your eyes.*

Then the men came back and lifted Jack. His head rolled forward and they dragged him toward the kitchen.

You have to move, thought Leo. The strength was rising in him — a moment of clarity.

You have to move.

You have to move.

You have to see what's in that kitchen.

Somehow Leo made it to his feet. He was moving through water and high wind. He and time were moving together. Slowly, incredulously, insidiously. Looking back, Leo saw Allissa slumped on the chair next to him. Her eyes were open. Could she move? Could she make it up? Her eyes were open. There was hope.

Allissa pushed forwards and stood clear of the table. She stumbled onto shaking legs.

Talking was still impossible.

Together they reached the kitchen door and supported themselves on the frame.

The door hadn't shut and a vertical bar of light seeped into the dark restaurant. Leo and Allissa peered through.

Jack slumped across the arms of the smaller waiter, his head hanging limp.

The men spoke in unrecognisable mutterings.

The larger man picked up one of the dishes — dark, thick, heavy metal. Leo and Allissa recoiled with the movement. The man held it up at an angle. There was no doubt what he was about to do.

The scene held as though drunk. The dish began to move through the air.

Focus on your breathing.

Breathe in, and out.

In and out.

Do not scream.

Two breaths in the silence.

Two breaths in the darkness.

One crack in the silence. The crack rang around the bare walls of the restaurant.

The man holding Jack dropped him to the floor. Blood ran down the edge of the dish and dripped into a pool. It spiralled from the gash on the back of Jack's head. Behind Jack, Miles' body lay face down. His thick limbs and grey hair, now only remnants of life.

Leo suppressed a gasp.

One waiter spoke and the other replied. They would come back into the restaurant at any moment. Leo and Allissa were going to have to run, and run now.

Leo knew he could run. His body was capable of it, if only he could get it to work.

Leo turned and half-dragged Allissa across the empty restaurant. They stumbled the first two paces, using the tables for support. They pushed through the door and out into the humid night. The waiters moved into the restaurant, their voices muffled by the door.

Leo and Alliss ran.

The voices behind them were raised now.

Leo focused on putting his feet on solid ground. He straightened up as his legs pumped. He held Allissa's arm and pulled her on.

They were running. The voices behind them shouted unknown words.

Leo and Allissa didn't stop to look. They ran, dodging piles of rubbish where they could, crashing through them when they couldn't. Leo had no idea where they were going. They turned right at a crossroads, then left, then right again.

Leo ran until his legs felt like knives. He ran until he tasted acid in his mouth. Then he ran some more. He was dragging Allissa, then being dragged by Allissa.

Each street was as dark as the last. Darker. Just another dusty alleyway lit by the occasional island of light. Faceless street after faceless street.

Neither turned to see if anyone followed. Neither knew how long they'd been running.

Finally Leo saw light ahead. The narrow street joined another. It was barely lit, but a beacon to eyes used to the darkness. They were moths running for the bulb. With light came safety.

The road they emerged on to was large by Kathmandu's standards. Lined with the closed shutters of shops. Like the rest of the sleeping city, it was now empty and quiet.

Leo and Allissa turned right and continued running. They needed to keep going. Running was to live. Stopping was to die.

Leo's vision fizzed. The road waned and jolted with each step. Twice he fell into the metal shutters of the closed shops and crashed to the floor. The sound of metal on metal echoed through the street. They groped their way forward using the shutters, parked cars, anything they could for support. They had to keep going.

They stumbled against a pink and white taxi and something stirred inside. Someone was asleep on the back seat. A man lay curled up beneath a blanket in the rear of the tiny vehicle. Leo banged on the glass. The man pulled the blanket up over his head.

Allissa pulled a wad of notes from a pocket and pressed them against the window.

The taxi driver glanced up. Still half-asleep, he climbed forward and unlocked the doors.

Leo yanked open the back door of the taxi, pushed Allissa in, and then fell in himself.

The taxi began to move and the city merged into a muddy scar of dark and light against the window. Leo heard voices, but right now, he didn't care. He was warm and comfortable and alive.

63

Every city is full of people working as hard as they can. The whole idea of cities started with people coming together for work. These people make and operate and move. They repair and fix and watch.

There are few places where this is more obvious than Kathmandu. Nothing is hidden in the mountain city. The roads are choked with lorries travelling for weeks through mountain passes to get something somewhere.

Sometimes these lorries don't make it. A miscalculated corner or a lapse of concentration is all it takes on a clifftop road. Tau, Jem and Jack saw painful reminders of this along the road from Pokhara. The carcasses of lorries, buses and cars lay hundreds of feet below after a slipped wheel or an overshot corner.

These machines must also be manned by people, and to transport them an army of tattered pink and white taxis surge through the streets day and night.

There are two types of taxi drivers in the city. One lives locally and often works in a pair. Perhaps brothers who sunk family savings into buying the battered car. One driver works the first twelve hours of the day, the other the second. They don't miss a moment of service between them. The second type are men who live further away. Their homes maybe ten or more hours drive from Kathmandu. These men work for months without a break, eating, sleeping and existing only in the car.

Imay is one of these taxi drivers. It's been three months since he's seen his family. He assures himself he will see his wife and two daughters again soon. There's a picture of them on the dashboard of his taxi. Every time he looks at it he's reminded why he has to be away.

He's just completed his final job of the night, taking a pair of tourists to the airport for an early morning flight. He knows there's very little trade between two and four in the morning. Finding a quiet spot, he parks the taxi to get some rest.

Imay climbs into the back of the taxi and wishes good-night to the photo of his family. He imagines their voices saying it in return. He makes sure his money belt is secure. There are many stories of taxi drivers being robbed while they sleep. The belt is getting fat — he must go to the bank soon.

He tucks a thin blanket around him and drifts into a restless sleep. He dreams of the smells of his village and the taste of the mist.

Minutes later, Imay is woken by a crash against the car. He opens his eyes. It's just a drunk tourist stumbling from one place to the next. They'll move on. He rearranges the blanket, twisting in the small rear seat to find the sweet spot.

Another bang. And another. Reluctantly, he opens his eyes. A man presses against the glass above him. A girl leans on the car beside him. The girl reaches into her pocket and pushes a handful of notes against the window — a lot of notes.

Imay looks at the picture of his wife and children, streaked by the shadows of the street. As much as he wants his sleep, this could get him home sooner.

He climbs into the driver's seat and unlocks the doors.

The girl gets in first. The man follows. They are both out cold before Imay has even started the car; their heads flop against the glass and they breathe deeply.

In the rearview mirror, Imay sees two men running towards him. Tall men. One carries some kind of weapon.

This is not good.

Whatever these guys want, it won't end well. Imay snaps the taxi into gear, then pulls out of the parking space and accelerates away. The men are left breathless in a skittering of dust. Imay knows there are thousands of taxis which look just like his. They'll never catch up with him.

But this does leave him with a problem. He has a pair of passed-out tourists in his taxi who are wanted by not very nice-looking men. Normally if someone falls asleep in his car, Imay finds a safe doorway and puts them there. But these two are in danger.

For their own good, he decides to take them to the police station. It'll cost him. He knows that. But, he's made good money from them. The least he can do is make sure they're safe.

The Kathmandu Central Police Station is less than ten minutes away. Pulling around the back and parking between two police cars, Imay goes inside to negotiate. He offers to split the fare with the policeman on duty, telling him the total was half what he was given. He leaves out the part with the two men chasing; that'll double the price and could cause trouble later.

Two police officers walk out with Imay. First, they take the man from the back seat. He's asleep. He's breathing heavily and muttering inaudible words. Then they come back for the girl. They carry her carefully, as though she's their sister.

Imay sits in the empty car and counts the notes. That's two extra days with his family.

64

Dawn broke over Kathmandu like a hangover. The sun forced itself above the highest clouds, lighting the city through millions of gallons of threatening rain and leaving a milky, grey, half-waking glow.

Allissa opened her eyes. Slowly.

Without moving, she checked the feeling in her limbs. All appeared to be as it should. Then, still without sitting up, she attempted to work out where she was. It certainly wasn't her bedroom – the thin mattress beneath her gave little protection from a hard surface. The authoritarian grey ceiling was striped with shadows. Footsteps echoed down a long, bare corridor. And voices. There were voices, too. Voices she could neither understand nor even hear properly.

She was going to have to sit up and see what was going on. Something told her it wouldn't be good.

Then, from somewhere close by, Allissa heard heavy breathing. Heavy gasps of breath. Desperate, ragged intakes of thick air, each one heavier than the last.

Allissa sat up, her head stinging with the movement. She

let the pain subside and looked around. They were in a cell — bare concrete and iron bars.

Leo sat on a bunk on the other side of the room. His head drooped between his legs as he gasped for air.

Allissa steadied herself and stood up shakily. She crossed the cell and sat beside Leo.

He was breathing sharply, each of his inhalations a mere snatch of air.

"You're going to be alright. You're safe," Allissa said, putting her hand on his back.

Leo looked up at her and tried to speak. "I... I..."

"No, don't speak just yet," Allissa said. She recognised the symptoms of panic.

"I just want you to concentrate on your breathing for a minute," she said. "You're having some kind of panic attack, but that will pass soon. You'll be okay. We're both safe. We're going to be okay, and we'll get out of here soon."

Leo's breathing eventually slowed and the muscles in his back, neck and arms relaxed.

"I think we've seen a murder," he said quietly.

Allissa thought back to the events of the previous evening. She sat back against the cold wall of the cell and tried to stitch her memories together. At first, they only came back in parts, like an overplayed video; Jack's limp body on the floor, the spiralling pool of blood, the dish moving through the air.

They had seen, Allissa thought, unable to finish the sentence. *They had seen —*

"A murder!" Leo shouted, getting to his feet and running to the bars of the cell. "We've seen a murder. You need to help us. Somebody help us!" He banged and screamed through the bars.

Leo was right. They had seen a murder. Two murders.

"We've seen a murder! Help! We need help!"

Leo's breathing became even more frantic as he shook the bars. A pair of police officers arrived. Leo continued to pant and shout, each breath becoming lighter. He dropped to his knees, gasping.

One of the officers unlocked the door.

"Murder. There's been a murder," Leo continued, yelling between gasps.

Allissa watched, detached from the events around her. It seemed like the hazy memory of a dream, as though it were all happening behind glass.

The two police officers glanced at each other. These tourists needed to be out before the shift change in half an hour.

One of the officers helped Leo to his feet, and the other approached Allissa. She calmly eased herself up with only the help of an outstretched hand.

"Murder. We've seen a murder. You have to help," Leo whispered.

The officers guided Leo and Allissa to a room and sat them on two metal chairs in the centre. One kept a hand on Leo's shoulder while the other fetched two cups of hot chai.

Without warning, the images of Jack and Miles spooled across Allissa's mind again. Although they were shocking, they felt like someone else's memories. It were as if she hadn't been there at all.

More officers arrived and one knelt down beside Leo.

"You have a good night, yes?" the officer said, smiling and glancing from Leo to Allissa.

"We've seen a murder. There were men chasing us. You have to help," Leo muttered.

"Say again, my English not good."

"I've seen a murder! Murder, killing!"

The officer thought intently for a few seconds, then stood to face the others. He said two words and the men broke into laughter. It was the sort of hearty, throaty, genuine laughter that couldn't be controlled. One man acted out smoking, then going weak at the knees while another mimed the stabbing of a colleague. One even slapped Leo on the back.

"You need to take this seriously!" Leo shouted. The officers bundled them up and led them back out into the grey corridor. "I'm not joking! I can show you where it happened!"

The officers' laughter subsided as Leo continued. They increased their pace toward the police station's exit.

The light stung Allissa's eyes as they emerged into the sluggish morning. At the roadside, one of the officers hailed a taxi and slid Leo and Allissa into the back seat.

As the taxi pulled away from the police station, Leo and Allissa looked at each other. They both knew what they'd seen, though neither could yet make sense of it.

Beyond the dust-streaked windows of the taxi, Kathmandu seemed different, distant and cruel. People were stirring into life, but instead of setting up for work, they pulled large plastic sheets between suspended cables and cleared drainage ditches. A storm was coming.

65

Leo had wanted to visit the Taj Mahal ever since he'd seen a timeless photo of it as a child. Each grainy black and white pixel hinted at exciting and undiscovered lands; stories of passion and pride; tales of hope and opportunity.

Now, as he and Mya get ready for an evening of food and drinks, with their plan to get up early to see the Taj at sunrise, his excitement builds.

He is here, they are here, and the world's greatest memorial to love and loss is less than a mile away. It's a day he knows will be unforgettable, especially with what he has planned. What could be better than asking the most important question of his life outside the monument which signifies love like no other in the world? He envisions it now, bent to one knee, the eminent marble domes of the Taj in the background as he presents Mya with the ring. The ring he's been hiding for the entire trip.

Will you... the words stutter in the turbulent anxiety of his mind. *Will you...*

As Mya takes a shower, Leo rummages through his bag

for the ring. It's been carefully buried amongst his stuff for almost a month now, but tonight he'll need to hide it close so that he can take it in the morning without her noticing.

Leo feels the felt-covered box at the bottom of his bag and pulls it out. He should probably leave the box here, as it would be easier to take the ring on its own. He snaps the box open and looks at the slender band of silver crowned with three angrily glinting diamonds.

What if they have metal detectors and bag searches on the way in? She can't see the ring before the moment is right.

"Shower's free," Mya says, walking into the bedroom wrapped in a towel. "It's warm, get in now."

"Thanks," Leo says, checking she can't see him before snapping the box closed and stuffing it in the backpack.

Tomorrow, he thinks. *Tomorrow will be perfect.*

They leave the hotel and walk side-by-side through Agra's hurried streets. The smells, colours and vibrancy of India surround them. It's a city like many others — throbbing traffic, spices, gabbling conversation. Up ahead, a long-horned cow saunters across the stream of tourists. Those new to Indian life reach for their cameras. Others sigh and wait for the unique delay to pass.

"Look at that," Mya says, pointing out a sign on a building to the left.

Rooftop bar and restaurant, views of Taj Mahal.

"Shall we?" she says, crossing the road before waiting for a reply.

They climb a dusty stairwell. Each floor contains a different guesthouse or residence. On the final flight, a strip of sky appears above them.

Then, standing on the skyline, amid the jumble and tussle of Agra, the Taj reveals herself. Domes and minarets in ivory white take on the changing hue of the glowing air.

Dazzling, shining, as they have every day for five-hundred years.

The day is almost up. The colours of the evening start to glow from the horizon, and long streaks of cloud spread like bunting. Leo and Mya are the only two in the rooftop bar. The noise of cutlery, distant chatter and the growl of the city are the only interruptions.

Mya turns to look at the Taj on the skyline. Leo looks at her as she does. Despite his lifelong desire to see the Taj, he knows it's just a building. Buildings don't give people hope, or optimism or love; they can inspire it, but those feelings come from others. Watching the pinks of the sky glow over her skin and the last of the sun shimmering in her deep, unblinking eyes, Leo loses focus on the marble mausoleum completely.

Why do we need to travel at all? It can't be because of the sights and sounds and smells of the place. You can see or smell things anywhere. Is it the people? Not really, because the world is full of people. You can meet new and interesting people every day.

Watching Mya blink away the dry evening, Leo knows it's because of the feeling. When you travel, you leave your feelings behind and open your heart and mind to the raw struggles of others. Whether that's the people you meet or those you travel beside.

He knows what to do.

"I've... I've left my phone back in the room," he says, touching Mya on the arm. "I'd really like to get a picture of this."

"Use mine if you —"

"Order me a beer," Leo says, already backing towards the stairs. "I'll be ten minutes."

Excitement prickles as he climbs the stairs a few

minutes later, the ring tucked into his wallet. He pauses on the final landing to get his breath back.

This is the moment. This is his moment. Their moment.

He prepares himself and takes the last few stairs slowly.

Breathe deeply.

In and out.

In and out.

The city's now just a murmur. No sound exists but the thumping of his heart and the words he wants to say so much.

Will you... Will you...

Leo reaches the top of the stairs and looks out across the bar.

Mya stands, watching the city.

But she's not alone. Another man stands with her. They're talking.

Leo steps back into the stairwell. A waiter clatters past him with a tray of drinks.

Mya turns to look at the man — he's young, striking, attractive. He puts a strong hand on her slender waist as they laugh together.

At that moment Leo realises something. You can't travel to change the world, but when you travel, you feel the world, whether that's the helplessness of Indian poverty or the true intentions of someone you love.

66

The light over Kathmandu turned from mango to aubergine as the rain started to pepper and fizz against the window of Leo's hotel room. Leo opened his eyes. He recognised the room from the web of cracks across the ceiling, the dust-ridden curtains and the grinding noise of the ceiling fan. He was fully clothed on top of the bed. Allissa slept soundly beside him. Her body curled tight, her breathing slow and deep.

The memories of the night before thumped into his thoughts: the lamb, the noxious smoke, the dish, Jack and Miles. Leo sat up on the bed and pulled his knees inwards.

"I don't know why you wanted to be a journalist anyway," Leo's mum had said at a family meal a few months ago. "I just can't see how you're right for that... It's not an insult," she said, seeing his dejected look. "You've always been so shy. I just can't imagine you interrogating someone in an interview."

She was right. What could he do? This just wasn't right for him. He couldn't do this. Who was he to think he could? The man who didn't like complaining in restaurants, now trying to solve a missing person's case? Now a murder? This wasn't him. It was a joke.

Leo looked around. He longed for the feeling of his now-distant flat. He wanted more than anything to collapse into his sagging sofa and look at the world through the soft, safe glow of a computer screen.

This wasn't him. This just wasn't him.

Allissa woke to the sound of movement in the room and opened her eyes slowly. The headache had gone, and although she felt grimy, her mouth furry and her tongue thick, she knew that would pass. She pulled herself upright. She was on the bed in Leo's hotel room, where she'd collapsed moments after arriving. On the other side of the room, Leo frantically stuffed clothes into a backpack.

"Going somewhere?" Allissa said croakily.

"I've got to get out of here," Leo said. "You should too. It's not safe. What we saw last night, that could have been us. I can't believe the police won't help us."

Leo swore under his breath as a bundle of t-shirts fell to the floor.

"We'll do something," Allissa said, lifting a glass of water from the bedside table. It didn't look fresh, but she took a sip all the same.

"No, we tried that this morning," Leo said, scooping up the clothes and stuffing them into the bag. "They laughed at us. We tried to help. I'm done with trying to help. I didn't get into this to witness people being killed. I'm getting out of here."

"Oh right, so you're just going? That's you done, is it?"

"Yeah, and you should get out of here too. I'm not trusting a place where even the police won't take me seriously."

"Well, we didn't turn up there in the best of states,"

Allissa said. Leo didn't stop to meet her eye. "Things do work a bit differently here. You've got to appreciate that —"

"I've got to appreciate that?" Leo raised his voice and looked at Allissa for the first time since waking. His eyes were red and bracketed with dark circles.

"Yeah, you've got to appreciate that. Think about it. If you have to be taken to a police station because you're on drugs, they're not going to be receptive to what you claim you've seen. Especially in Kathmandu. This city has seen a lot of drugged up westerners in its time."

Leo propped the bag against the wall and grabbed another pile of clothes.

"We were drugged," he said finally, but with less conviction than before.

"Well yes, but they didn't know that," Allissa said coolly. "I'm not saying we do nothing. I'm just saying it's pretty obvious they weren't going to believe us this morning."

Leo looked from Allissa to the window.

"I can't," he said finally. "I came here to find you. I've found you. Now I'm going." Leo pulled the rucksack onto his shoulder and opened the door. He paused and looked back at Allissa. "I'll tell your family you're safe and well. Don't worry, I won't tell them where you are."

"Do what you like," Allissa replied.

67

Kathmandu airport smelled of lemon and damp. The building, a mid-twentieth century reminder of what Kathmandu was trying to be, teemed with people all wanting to leave the city. Although the storm was yet to arrive, wind and rain slashed against the windows. The skies around the mountain city swirled with electricity and anticipation. No flights had left since the night before, choosing the safety of the ground over the turbulent air.

Most people sat bright and optimistic, chatting on benches or together on the floor. These were people at the start of their journeys. To them, the storm represented just another travelling story.

The harder it is to get there, the better it'll be when we do.

For others, those midway through a long journey, that spirit had long since disappeared. They wore the look of battery hens — each moment of rest indicated by electric light and opportunity rather than the cycle of days.

At the back of the brightly-lit international departures hall, a smaller space for local flights sat in darkness. The few lights that did work mimicked the flashes in the sky outside. The room was quiet; no flights would be leaving from this terminal in the coming days. The smaller planes had been taken off the runway and stored in their hangars some time ago. Even being exposed on the ground during the storm could damage their fragile bodies.

Leo sat between a sign advertising flights to the Himalayas and a humming vending machine stripped of its contents. Having discovered that all outbound flights were cancelled, his brain throbbed. He sat on a bench, head in his hands, his mind swirling and pounding like the storm outside.

He needed to go. He needed to get out of this city. He wasn't the sort of person who could do this. Coming here had been a terrible idea.

Focus, calm, breathe.

Leo counted his breaths as self-doubt closed in.

Why had he thought this was a good idea? He couldn't do this. This wasn't him.

He stared morosely at the grime-darkened floor.

It wasn't the thought of Jack, the moving dish or the spiralling pool of blood that bothered him the most. Neither was it the restaurant, the chase or the police.

Breathe in and out. Calm, focus, clarity.

All he could think about — all that plagued his mind, twisting and clouding his thoughts to such an extent that he felt tightness occupy his chest — was Allissa.

Allissa.

Finding her had been his success. He'd done it. Only for it to go so badly, so wrong.

Should he have seen it coming? Could he have done any more? He knew cities could be dangerous, they always were. But how could he have known this was going to happen?

Breathe in and out. Calm, focus, clarity.

But Allissa? He'd found her. That was a success, right? That was his only success, and that troubled him. Why had he found Allissa, only to almost lose her again? Beneath the worry, self-doubt and anxiety, an instinct rumbled. An instinct which, despite everything else, demanded attention.

Something just didn't seem right. The question was — why had he succeeded in finding Allissa, when everything else had gone so wrong?

Allissa was the exception that proved the rule. She was his one success. His only success in the last week, in the last year. Maybe ever.

Why, how, had he succeeded in finding her, only to fail at everything else?

Something Allissa said the day before floated into his mind.

The taillights of a plane crossed the tarmac beyond the rain-streaked windows.

Just you wait, she'd told him, *he'll have a plan.*

68

Flying never bothered Marcus Green. As part of his job, he'd flown across the world numerous times, frequently to unwelcoming places and under hostile conditions. But the flight into Kathmandu's airport that evening, his knuckles draining of blood on the armrest, was one he knew he'd remember.

Green braced for landing in the buffeting plane as streaks of lightning flashed past the windows. He knew that planes wouldn't usually land in these conditions, but to get across the mountains again would be even more dangerous. Green peered out into the darkness and watched the underbelly strobes flicker through the clouds. The red light on the end of the wing came into view. It seemed to twist and buckle through the impenetrable air.

A thunderous crack echoed through the cabin. The lights blinked on and off, and one of the overhead lockers sprung open. Green gasped, imagining the plane ploughing into the side of a mountain. Then, hearing the roar of the engines as they thrusted to slow, he realised they'd landed.

The distant glow of the terminal building materialized through the fog.

Green wiped a hand across his damp forehead. They had arrived.

A few minutes later, he and the other passengers were herded out into the driving rain. A man in a bright yellow jacket hurried them into the terminal building.

Once inside, Green dug out his phone and connected it to the local network. He needed to get in touch with the team back in London as soon as possible. He was lucky to have made it to Kathmandu. Two days in a hotel in Mumbai had been the other option. Now he had work to do.

Green drifted through baggage reclaim and immigration as the adrenaline drained. He checked his phone several times. Nothing. In place of the network icon, two arrows spun around each other. It wasn't until he walked toward the doors leading out into the rain-lashed evening that his phone finally beeped.

An email from his editor glowed promisingly in the inbox. Green hoped it was news from the research. The circus of the terminal dropped to a faint hubbub around him as he read.

No wonder Stockwell wanted this hidden, Green thought, his eyes wide. *This isn't just him losing his job and reputation. This is prison.*

69

Leo wanted to leave Kathmandu. Yet, Kathmandu wasn't finished with him. The weather had closed in. No planes would be leaving for a while.

The storm wasn't the only one with a score to settle, Leo thought, heading for the doors.

"Man, how are ya? What's happening?" Tau's voice seemed distant as he answered Leo's call. Leo could hardly hear him over the rattle of the taxi and the pounding rain.

"Yeah, so much to tell you," Leo said, leaning back into the seat as the taxi accelerated. The lights of the city were just a blur behind the glass.

"I thought so, as I hadn't heard from you all day," Tau said.

Leo swallowed hard, trying not to be irritated by the insinuation. The taxi slid around a corner. The weather, poor visibility and soaking roads were clearly no reason to slow down.

"Nah, listen, it's not good," Leo shouted into the phone against the rattling rain. "Meet me at Allissa's guesthouse. It's not good. I'll explain when I see you."

Tau agreed, and Leo disconnected the call.

Leo had thought he was leaving Kathmandu. Now the city was swallowing him once more. As he had nearly a week before, Leo watched the buildings streak past.

Yet again, he had a job to do. The only difference? This time he knew exactly what it was.

70

A bulb began to blaze in the dark sprawl of back street passageways. To those who knew, it advertised the restaurant was open for business.

The passage was dark. The heavy leaden sky crushed light from the city long before it was due. To the men in the backstreet restaurant preparing meat for their evening service, the day was like any other. Tourists would still make it out; they always did. Tonight, Himalayan Lamb was on the menu for the crowd who filled the dark dining room.

Moths started to orbit the bulb above the door. For forty years the light had called to the insects who darted around it — dirty creatures who just followed their instincts. The restaurant did the same for the travelling vagrants who ate behind the grimy door. That was how the brothers contrived their living. If someone needed to be made to disappear in Kathmandu, they just needed to find their way to the restaurant. There was a fee, of course, but it was reasonable. Especially considering the brothers handled everything, including disposal.

The brothers talked casually as they prepared the meat

for tonight's dinner service. Short, sharp knives moved expediently. Bone separated from muscle and fat split from flesh. The men needed to hurry. Customers would arrive soon. They would expect the famous Himalayan Lamb.

They were concerned about the two that got away. It was unexpected and unacceptable. The customer, the man they only knew by voice, would be disappointed. It was a loose end, and that was bad for everyone.

The brothers had considered staying closed for a few days to let things settle. But they decided that wouldn't be necessary. It wasn't like the two who got away would remember anything. The drugs in the smoke made sure of that.

The phone on the wall pierced the silence.

The smaller of the two brothers answered. Blood dripped from his hands.

"Is it done?"

"We kill two of them," the brother said. The line crackled.

"Did you kill the girl and the young man with the long hair?"

He didn't fully understand the question. Thirty years of working in a restaurant had only taught him English in patches.

"Old man and young man."

The silence on the line fizzed across five thousand miles.

"You didn't kill a girl?"

"No."

"What happened to the girl?"

"She gone."

The line disconnected.

71

Allissa stood at the sink in the small kitchen of the Teku Guesthouse and watched the storm lash the city. She filled the sink with warm water and admired the rain-filtered view. Somehow it felt comforting. It was as though the rest of the city got to see life from her perspective for once.

Allissa returned to the guesthouse just before the rain started. Chimini and Fuli greeted her with anxious hugs and questions. They'd been worried about her when she didn't come home. She'd promised she was alright. There was nothing wrong. She'd just got carried away.

They'd eaten dinner together and laughed as usual. Allissa tried to join in from behind her glaze of detachment.

The warm water filled the sink and Allissa washed the plates. Two more guests had arrived that afternoon — a pair of young women staying for three nights. Chimini and Fuli were excited about it. It was good news. They now had real money coming in. Money to eat and live and survive. Maybe even thrive.

Allissa enjoyed the smiles through which Chimini and

Fuli spoke, but felt nothing herself. She wanted to feel excited with them. She couldn't. No emotion could permeate the wall of water which seemed to distort everything.

"Hello, Allissa?" A voice snapped her from the despondent daydream. It was a voice she recognised. "Allissa," Leo said, leaning on the reception desk.

Allissa watched him cooly as she dried her hands on a towel. She fought the urge to feel pleased, relieved or even hug him for coming back.

"They shouldn't have been killed," Leo said, sitting at the kitchen table. "It was meant for us. You said that your dad always had a plan, that he would be one step ahead. I was thinking about it at the airport. I'd only succeeded at one thing. Finding you. That's only because it's what your dad wanted me to do."

"Why would he need you, though?" Allissa asked.

"He had to send someone he knew you'd trust. Otherwise, you'd never have come out of hiding. So, he chose me. I'm not threatening. I was just trying to do the right thing. He knew you'd appreciate that and trust me. You'd feel like you had the upper hand."

Allissa nodded. Her eyes widened. "But how?"

"He must have had someone watch me. I would be easy to follow, and I'd lead them straight here."

"The Australian guy?"

"That's what I thought. It was all part of a plan. It was all worked out. We've been played."

"There was something about him. It was all just —"

"Too obvious?"

"Yeah, that's it. I bet all the stories he told were invented to get us to trust and go with him."

"Exactly," Leo said. "He probably had a nasty backup plan if we didn't go willingly."

"The guys there just hadn't counted on us barely touching the shisha."

"Yeah, they didn't think we'd escape," Leo said as Allissa's scowl softened.

"But it means they know we're still alive. They'll have told my dad by now, and he'll have a backup plan for sure."

Leo nodded. Could it already be too late?

A clatter from the reception area drew their attention.

Leo was first to his feet. He lifted the chair and held a finger to his lips.

Allissa stood. It felt strange for her to let someone else go first. She pushed the feeling of powerlessness aside. Leo had come back, and now they were looking out for each other.

Her eyes darted around the kitchen for something to use as a weapon. A block of knives glimmered from the counter.

Leo reached the door, opened it to a crack, and peered through.

72

"How have you found your first travelling experience?" Mya asks.

Nearly a month has passed since they'd arrived in Mumbai — an assault of noise and colour. They'd travelled north through the desert and palaces of Rajasthan to the teeming hub of Delhi. From there, they journeyed to Pushkar, Agra and Varanasi for a trip down the swollen Ganges. Then boarded the train to Goa for five days of walking on the beach, gorging on fresh fish and sipping late-night cocktails.

The white sand looks like it could run on forever. Restaurants with big wicker chairs display the day's catch on tables of ice. Hawkers move amongst the lounging tourists selling bangles, necklaces or bits of string which promise to bring the wearer good luck.

"Hey, tall man."

"Where you from?"

"Manchester United, yeah?" they shout, starting conversations with anyone inexperienced enough not to ignore them.

Further up the beach, a herd of cows break through the undergrowth and walk sedately between the chairs and tables. Tourists photograph the unique spectacle, impossible to imagine anywhere else in the world. The beasts drop to the sand and warm their backs in the fading sun.

"What's been your favourite part?" Mya asks.

"That's hard. It's all been so good. Just been an incredible month," Leo says, swigging on a bottle of beer. "You know what? I think the last few days have been the best... Yeah. I loved seeing the Taj Mahal, and I loved the trip down the Ganges and all that, but there's just been something incredible about being here. It's such a beautiful place."

A warm breeze pushes through the restaurant, causing the dark red cloth over a neighbouring table to shiver. It brings the smell of sandalwood and tropical undergrowth.

"It has been really special," Mya says. "I've always wanted to come to India. Are you ready to go home?"

"It feels so far away right now," Leo answers.

"Yeah, but do you want to go back there?" she pushes.

"No, I suppose not. We've been away so long, this feels like my life now."

Mya is beautiful, Leo thinks. Her dark hair has grown in the last month, and she's taken to tying it high on the back of her head with brightly-coloured headbands bought on the way. Her skin glows, boasting the tan of the last month, which makes her teeth and eyes shine.

Now would be a good time. The ring's been in his wallet for the last two weeks.

"Yeah, that's what I feel too," she says, reaching across the table and taking his hand in hers.

"Where would you like to go now, if you could?" Leo asks.

"I'd go down to Vietnam, then across to Thailand. There

are loads of places I've always wanted to see there. More temples. Beautiful food. The islands. From there I'd go across to China, starting in Hong Kong."

Mya turns to face the ocean. Leo watches the reflection of the setting sun in her eyes. The moment is perfect.

The words that Leo wants to say desert him and his breath draws tight. It's normally a feeling he associates with panic. Right now, it's exhilarating and invigorating.

He takes a deep breath and holds it.

This is the moment. His moment. Their moment.

"There's something I'd like to say to you," he says. Mya turns to look at him.

"There's something I need to tell you too," she replies. "Can I go first?"

Leo swallows and nods.

"I might as well just say it. I've wanted to tell you for a few days, but haven't found the moment." Mya glances at their hands.

Leo's mind roams.

"We're not going home tomorrow..."

"What do you mean?" Leo says.

"You know how to start with we were going to come here for two months and travel on to Vietnam afterwards? But you couldn't get the time off work."

"Yeah,"

"I knew you would like it so much that you'd want to carry on for two months. So even though you said no, I booked it."

Silence falls over the couple. The sun continues its laboured descent toward the Indian Ocean.

Leo doesn't know what to say or think. He just stares at Mya.

"Hold on, let me get this right," he says finally. "We're booked to go somewhere else tomorrow? Not home?"

"Yes. I've booked it all. We fly to Hanoi, then we're going to travel down to Ho Chi Minh City and then fly across to Thailand for five days on a beautiful island. Then we go home."

Again, words fail him. How has she done this? How has she done this and not told him?

"You didn't know how much things cost anyway, so I just told you it was the amount for two months when I booked it."

"But... but... I'm supposed to go back to work in three days," Leo says.

"I know," Mya replied. "But ultimately, Leo, that place has treated you so badly. They never give you the opportunities you deserve. They work you so hard for rubbish money. You deserve more."

Leo knows there's an element of truth in what she says, but it sounds like an insult. He hates the thought of her lying to him, deceiving him, travelling all this way, spending all this time with him, holding this secret.

Mya watches Leo, as though challenging him to argue.

"I'm sorry for lying to you. I just knew that once you were here, you wouldn't want to go home. I was right."

"That's not the point!" Leo's anger rises. "You can't just do that. You can't always have it your way. I said I could only do a month. You should have respected that. I know you don't like my job, I get that, you've said that before. But that's my choice to make." He looks towards the ocean. He doesn't want to meet her eye. "I'm going for a walk along the beach." Mya gets up. "No, you stay here," he says. "I need to work out what to do."

"I wanted to come for two months," Mya says bitterly, looking at Leo as he stands. "You said you could only do one because of that shitty job. You might want to ruin your life with paycheques and bullshit, but that's not me."

Without replying Leo walks toward the purring ocean.

73

The reception area of the Teku Guesthouse was in darkness as Leo peered out. Despite the gloom, he could make out a figure climbing the stairs. The person after them had moved quickly. They must have predicted that he and Allissa would be at the guesthouse.

Leo glanced back into the kitchen. A block of knives gleamed from the counter behind him. If needed he could be there in a second.

Leo's fear subsided as the figure moved into the light.

"Tau!" Leo said, opening the door. "Come in here."

Tau sat quietly as Leo and Allissa explained.

He was shocked by the death of someone he'd got to know well over the last few weeks. He also knew now wasn't the time to mourn and reflect. Not when danger was present and looming.

"We need to get out of here, now," Leo said.

"I know a hotel," Tau said, following Leo to the door. "I know the owner. He'll let us have rooms without officially checking in."

"That's good," Leo said. "If Stockwell has official connections, then he may be able to see the records."

"It's unlikely," Tau said.

"But it is possible," Allissa interrupted. "I know my dad. He'll be pissed off it didn't go to plan. He won't leave it there, that's for certain."

Leo killed the kitchen light and followed Tau and Allissa out into the reception area. A few days ago, Tau had been his only contact in the city, and Leo had trusted him through necessity. Tau's reaction in the last few minutes, however, made Leo trust him through respect, and that was something more. Leo couldn't think of anyone he would rather rely on.

The rain had intensified in the last half an hour. It had time to make up for. Leo squinted through the downpour as they crossed the square. The road shimmered beneath the sheets of water.

Tau flagged down a taxi and explained their destination to the driver. The taxi ebbed back into the sporadic flow of cars. The wipers whipped across the screen but failed to clear the glass.

As the taxi pulled up at a set of traffic lights, Tau turned to look through the rear window. He examined the headlights of the car behind through the soaking glass. Tau pulled a note from his pocket and spoke to the driver. The driver accepted the note, tucked it beneath the steering wheel, then accelerated through the red light.

"Watch the car behind," Tau said. "If they're following us, they'll have to pull out too."

Leo, Allissa and Tau turned in their seats. The car behind sat motionless for an instant before lurching through the lights too.

"Thought so," Tau declared. "They must have been sitting outside the guesthouse."

Leo and Allissa exchanged apprehensive glances.

"Don't worry, we'll sort it," Tau said, picking up his phone and making a call.

They drove for ten minutes in nervous silence. The whining engine and the drumming of the rain were the only sounds inside the taxi. Leo glanced at Allissa, who sat expressionless beside him.

"Sort the money now," Tau said, turning to Leo. "We've got to get out quickly."

Leo drew two notes from his wallet and handed them across. Tau put one in his pocket and handed the other to the driver.

The taxi pulled to the side of the road and stopped abruptly. Tau shouted some final instructions to the driver and leapt from the car. Allissa followed with Leo behind, his bag hanging awkward and heavy.

Once in the pummelling rain, Tau ran a few steps to a small door. It was just a shadow on the dark building. He started to knock.

Leo turned to see the taxi pull away and another car stop at the kerb. He tried to see through the car's dark windows — he wanted to know what they were up against. The passenger door opened, and the back of a head appeared above the car. Then Leo felt a draft of warm air as he was dragged inside.

Tau shut and locked the door behind them. They were in a small, dark room. Shelves stacked high with old TV sets covered every wall. Leo saw a hundred reflections of himself in their dulled, bulbous screens.

Tau greeted a small, grey-haired man.

"This is Baij," Tau said, "a friend of my father's."

"Follow me," Baij said, beckoning them through the shop and into a small back room. A dissected television sat on the table. It looked strange and antiquated, glimmering in the gloom. Baij pointed to the back door. Tau pushed it open and ran into the passage behind the building.

The passage was similar to the one Leo and Allissa had escaped through the previous night. Just a few feet in width, it ran down behind the buildings. Above them, tangled empty washing lines sagged like a giant spider's web. Drainpipes sang with water which sprayed out around ill-fitting joints.

The trio made quick progress down the passage. The height of the buildings protected them from the rain. Tau led, Allissa was second carrying her small bag high on her back, and Leo followed. With every step, his rucksack dug into his aching shoulders.

The passage joined the main road ahead. Cars flickered past.

"He's there already," Tau shouted, pointing ahead and quickening his pace. The taxi they had just left pulled to the side of the road. Tau broke into a run and Allissa followed. They swerved past stacked rubbish, boxes and empty gas canisters. Leo pulled the bag tight around his shoulders, clenched his teeth and ran too.

Tau reached the taxi first and lept into the passenger seat. Allissa climbed into the back and shuffled over to make room for Leo. Leo swung his bag in first and jumped in beside it.

The taxi driver grinned with camaraderie at Tau and then turned to the others. Tau pulled the other note from his now soaking jeans and passed it over.

In the back, Allissa and Leo stared wide-eyed and panting through the rear window.

Behind them, a lorry blocked half the road. Despite the torrents of rain, two men worked to repair it. Even in the reduced traffic of the evening, a queue had built up. The waiting drivers protested uselessly on their horns.

Unseen by the three in the car, a bedraggled figure appeared from behind the truck. Frustrated with the hold-up, he'd got out and ran around the corner just in time to see the taxi containing his quarry disappear through the sheets of rain.

74

M ya stands and heads towards the bar. The Goan sun has now almost sunk below the ocean. Lights start to twinkle in the restaurants and bars along the wide strip of sand.

Two men drinking at another table watch her as she passes.

Leo's been walking for five minutes. *How could she do this to me? It's my job. She can't just expect me to leave. That's a big decision. Jobs are important. Money makes the world go round.*

Hearing the voice in his mind, Leo suddenly doesn't recognize it.

These are the attitudes that have kept him trapped in his job, he realises all at once. A job that isn't going anywhere. Yet, here he is, punishing the person — angry with the person — who's trying to show him the breadth of the world.

He stops walking and looks around. Yes, work is important, but the woman he loves and the moments they share exploring the world — they're more important. So what if he pisses off a couple of guys in a dusty newspaper office on the other side of the world? He has everything he needs right here.

Leo's anger drifts away with the sweep of a wave. He pauses, then he turns back toward Mya.

He knows the smile Mya will give him when she sees him. A knowing beam which says, *welcome back, I'm glad you've decided to agree with me.*

Leo lifts his eyes toward the chairs spread out on the sand and looks for Mya's outline. He can't see her. Where is she? Getting closer, the place they'd been sitting comes into view. He can picture her there. But she isn't. It's their table. His shoes beneath his chair, his half-finished beer. No Mya.

Leo scans the restaurant and sees her sitting at a table talking to two guys. She leans back and drinks from a fresh bottle of beer. Jealousy rises again. *Assert yourself, go and get her.*

But he doesn't. He takes his seat and watches the wrestling ocean.

75

Leo and Allissa slept especially well. They'd entered their top floor rooms and had fallen straight into the dreamlessness of necessity after two virtually sleepless days. The rooms were basic. It was all they needed.

It was reassuring that the owner had greeted them in the foyer and promised the discretion they needed. He was happy to fill three empty rooms. Leo paid in cash, and everything remained out of the official records. They had the comfort they needed to sleep while the storm wreaked its relentless havoc.

The following morning Leo looked out of the window. The storm had subsided, and the city now looked fresh and clean. The dust had been stripped from the buildings, and the thick, congealing clouds had cleared. A sky of blameless blue with high strips of candyfloss white now enclosed the city. Leo gazed at the bright cityscape and realised it was the first time he had seen anything he liked about Kathmandu. He noticed a bright red flag on the roof of the building next door. It fought hard against its rope in the wind which had cleared the storm. Then he noticed another two on the buildings behind, those two yellow and white. Two more on a building to the right; blue and red. The more he looked, the more he saw. He strained his eyes to focus on the furthest flag he could, just a hint of light blue sparkling in the distance. Then he looked up toward the streak of clouds across the horizon. As they came into focus, Leo realised they weren't clouds at all, but the snow-covered crowns of the Himalayas. It was the first time Leo had seen mountains of that size, especially rearing above the city sprawl.

For centuries the city existed because of the mountains, because people from those mountains needed somewhere to work, or live, or trade. Usually all three. Although many people came to Kathmandu through choice, Leo knew that some were forced. Like the women Allissa helped, who had evaded their captors but still had nowhere to go. Women who had been lied to, cheated and imprisoned, to whom Allissa was bringing hope. Allissa had told Leo how the authorities were trying to stop these men, who promised young women great opportunities if they came to the city. Promises which disappeared the moment they arrived.

Leo stepped back from the window. His brow tightened in concentration. The idea was forming. They could blow this wide open, and make sure the men at the restaurant never hurt anyone again.

"I know how we can sort this," Leo said when he met Allissa and Tau for breakfast. The patio behind the hotel was quiet, and the bright sky bathed them in previously unknown warmth.

"It will be dangerous," Allissa said. "Particularly for you." She looked at Tau.

"Those men are evil, right?" Tau said.

"Yeah," Leo agreed. "They're killers."

"Then this is my opportunity to do something good. In a

way, I've been waiting a long time for this. People have done good things for me. This is my way to give back."

Leo realised how little he knew about Tau. When this was over, Leo promised himself he would get to know Tau better before they parted.

"How do you feel about involving the girls at the guest-house?" Tau asked Allissa.

"Chimini and Fuli? Not great."

"Do you think they'll do it?"

"Yes. That's the problem. They trust me, so they'll do anything I ask. But I'm not sure it'll be good for them. Particularly Fuli."

"They'll be helping bring some bad people to justice, hopefully," Leo said. "And they won't come to any harm. We'll make sure of that."

Allissa smiled weakly.

"No harm will come to either of them," Tau said. "That I can guarantee you."

"What about my dad?" Allissa asked.

"He's no doubt got people coming after us," Leo said, looking at Allissa. "Once we've made sure those men have paid properly for their crimes, I say we get out of the city."

"Hello, hello," came an anxious voice from the door. Leo, Tau and Allissa turned as the hotel owner hurried toward them.

"A man has been asking for you. He has a picture of you." He pointed to Allissa. "I said I have never seen you, and he left. But this must not be good news. There is someone looking for you."

They exchanged glances

"He's obviously just going around hotels asking," Leo reassured them. "If he knew we were here, he wouldn't be asking. He'd just have come in."

"He left this." The hotelier handed Tau a business card with a phone number scrawled on it.

"How much was he offering?" Leo asked.

"Fifty dollars."

"Cheapskate!" Leo blurted. "I'll give you twice that for saying nothing."

"You are my guests and my friends. I would never betray your trust like that," the owner said urgently.

"Of course, I did not mean —"

"He didn't mean that," said Tau. "He means that he may give you one hundred dollars for two more nights, if we decide to stay."

Leo didn't argue as the hotelier shuffled away.

"This makes things a little easier," Allissa said, reaching over and taking the card from Tau. "We can just invite him along to our little gathering later."

Leo felt a grin start to form.

"We need to make sure this guy isn't not watching the hotel, " Tau said, lifting himself from the chair. "He won't know who I am, so I'll check. You two stay inside until I'm back."

Leo and Allissa watched Tau disappear inside.

The drone of traffic was distant here. There seemed to exist places in the city where the noise was quieter, although it was always there. The intensity of the dust and pollution in the air had subsided with the storm, though.

"How long have you suffered panic attacks?" Allissa asked.

Leo looked at her. She squinted in the bright sunshine.

"Panic attacks? Nah, it's nothing, honestly." Leo belittled the thought with a flick of his hand.

"It didn't seem like nothing. You were in a pretty bad way."

"Well, yeah, we had been through a pretty horrible experience."

"I know, but that wasn't the first panic attack you've had, was it?"

Leo glanced at his empty coffee cup.

"It's nothing to be ashamed or embarrassed about."

"I suppose, but —"

"It's not at all. You're not letting it stop you do things. That's what's important."

"It's annoying." Leo thought of all the times he'd refused to go out with friends because of the embarrassment he would feel should one come on at that time. "A couple of years ago I thought I'd got rid of them completely. Then when Mya, you know... They came back."

"You just need to know how to cope with them," Allissa said, her warm smile more supportive than her words could ever be. "You need to know that you'll survive and that they don't make you any less strong."

Leo looked at her.

"When the time comes," Allissa said, putting a hand on his arm, "I'd trust you to do the right thing. That's what counts."

76

"I'll arrange for her to be taken there, yes."

Stockwell's voice came through Green's earpiece as he sat in the hotel's grand dining room.

Green had heard the recorded message dozens of times now and knew it word for word. It was the closest he'd come to actually speaking with Stockwell. He was listening again now that he was in Kathmandu to see if it held any more meaning. Sometimes things just made sense when you heard them in a different place.

It wasn't working this time. He still couldn't work out where Stockwell wanted Allissa to go, who was doing it for him, or when it was supposed to happen.

Green rubbed his eyes and finished the small cup of coffee. He caught the attention of a passing waiter and ordered a refill. More than one cup would be necessary today, with last night's sleep totaling minutes rather than hours.

Arriving at the hotel late, Green had met with his team of informants. The men, sorted for him by a contact, were his eyes and ears around the city. All spoke relatively good

English, but by the time he had briefed them and checked they understood, it was very late indeed. He told each contact that they should contact him if they saw or heard anything that might be useful.

There had been no word yet.

"Yes, she's already in Kathmandu," the recording said.

But *where* in Kathmandu was she? That's what Green needed to know. And soon. He didn't have much time. Nor did Allissa.

Scrolling through his phone, Green brought up the picture of the Stockwell family. In the picture, Allissa looked off to the right of the frame. *Where are you?* Green thought, *and what do you know?*

"It'll be tonight or tomorrow. You need to look out for her," came Stockwell's voice again.

This case was so close to being tied up, Green knew it. He had almost everything he needed. He just needed to find Allissa before her father did.

"I need to know you'll do everything. There can't be any loose ends."

Green winced at the nonchalance.

"No loose ends."

77

Dusk was falling as Tau and Fuli walked beneath the swinging bare bulb and into the restaurant. Trying his best to look like a tourist, Tau toted a bag which Fuli and Chimini had brought from the guesthouse.

Finding the restaurant again had been a miracle. Leo and Allissa were confident they would be able to if they came from the bar with the Chinese lanterns, despite it being dark when they made the journey last time. Unreassuringly, they couldn't agree as to whether it was left, left and left again, or left, left, then right. Somehow though, with minimal wrong turns, they made it.

Fuli kept three paces behind Tau, making no attempt to disguise the fact she didn't want to be there. She was doing this for Allissa.

Initially, they'd discussed Tau going alone, then decided that was too dangerous. Someone should be there to run for help if necessary. It would also look more natural if Tau had company. Although tourists often travelled to Kathmandu alone, they usually ate and drank in groups. It was to be

Fuli's testimony that would seal the fate of the men, so a good description of them and the restaurant was essential.

Despite the descending dusk outside, Tau's eyes needed to adjust as he stepped through the door.

A waiter crossed the restaurant and greeted Tau and Fuli in English and Nepalese. Tau caught his gaze and shuddered. This man was a killer. The waiter indicated an available table and slid off to take an order.

Tau positioned himself on one side of the small table. The restaurant was busy. It was impressive that so many people could be seated in such a small space. They lounged on stools, which the locals made look comfortable and the tourist found too small. Tau tried to start a conversation to reassure Fuli, but she ignored him. It didn't matter to Tau. He wasn't there for the conversation. He was there to do a job. It was going to be easy in a place this size. He needed to move without being seen by the waiters. Timing would be everything.

Tau watched the waiter move from one group of customers to the next. Tau couldn't stop thinking of the expression on the waiter's face as they'd entered the restaurant. The unblinking, watery eyes of a killer. A killer they were going to bring to justice. Tau slid the bag from his shoulder and positioned it between his legs. He would wait for the right moment and get out as soon as possible.

Leo and Allissa waited outside; they couldn't risk being seen by the men. Allissa had suggested that she and Leo go in, on account that the waiters probably wouldn't try anything when the restaurant was open. Tau and Leo thought it was a risk they couldn't take.

The pair stood in a shaded doorway less than thirty metres from the restaurant's unassuming entrance. The passage was narrow, but the inset doorway concealed them if they stood with their backs to the wall. If they were needed, they could be there in seconds.

The infamous bare bulb swung gently on its wire above the door. Moths gathered in the faltering daylight.

It was fortunate the restaurant was busy, Tau thought as he looked around. There was less chance the men would see him if they were talking to customers.

One of the waiters took an order from a group of tourists at the back of the room, his already curt service turning to irritation with the barrage of constant questions. Tau needed to wait for both waiters to be distracted. Leo had said there were only two. Tau hoped he was right.

Tau shuffled the bag beneath the table. He needed to leave it somewhere customers wouldn't go. Its contents would corroborate the testimony Fuli was going to give, and provide enough evidence for police to look very closely at the restaurant. The best bet would be the kitchen, as the men could just blame it on a customer if it was in the dining room.

The second waiter walked into the dining room. They looked so alike, they had to be brothers. The waiter carried two long metal bowls of steaming, sizzling meat.

Tau gripped the bag; this could be his opportunity.

Tau stood and moved across the dining room. He paused and turned to see where the waiters were. Leo and Allissa had assured him no one else worked in the restaurant.

The larger of the two waiters continued to take orders with his back to the kitchen. He poked violently at a menu. The other waiter rounded the final corner with the two trays of steaming meat. His back was now to the kitchen door too.

Tau pushed open the door and stepped quietly into the kitchen.

Bright lights glared from overhead strips and steel counter-tops glimmered.

Tau had to work quickly. He didn't have much time.

Two half-prepared meals waited on the counted. A large cut of meat glistened with spices. A white bone poked from the centre.

Sounds from the restaurant echoed through the door.

Tau needed to find a good place to leave the bag. Somewhere it wouldn't be seen until the police found it. Most of the storage spaces were open. The bag would be seen in seconds there. He had to hide it somewhere.

Tau moved through the kitchen, looking around. A large storage area lay to the right. Shelves contained herbs and spices. Two large fridges hummed in the quiet room.

Noise babbled from the restaurant behind him. A plate clattered to the floor. The drunken, laughing voices of tourists raised together.

Beyond the shelves, half-hidden in a shadowy corner, stood a piece of furniture totally out of place in the gleaming kitchen. A wooden cupboard. Ornate, classical, and carved from fine wood. Tau didn't know what to expect inside. Possibly chef's whites, or the dark outfits the two men in the restaurant wore? Tau opened the door. He certainly didn't expect to see what lay within.

In the cupboard hung a variety of clothes. Different colours, sizes and styles. T-shirts, trousers, shorts, bright shirts, long shirts, short ones. He pulled one from the far right-hand side. It was a large, bright blue shirt which hung lower than most. It wasn't until he pulled it out that he noticed the dark stain across the front.

From behind him, Tau heard the door of the kitchen swing open.

78

Allissa hated doing nothing. She felt useless standing in the doorway, knowing that someone else was solving the problem she and Leo had gotten themselves into.

"I wish they'd hurry up," she whispered. "I feel terrible asking Fuli to do this. She's been through enough."

Leo nodded.

"She's in no danger though. Any issues, she'll be straight out here."

Two pairs of eyes were fixed on the door, the swinging bulb and the circling moths.

———

TAU STEPPED BACK into the shadow beside the cupboard. He'd considered trying to climb in amongst the clothes, but didn't think the cupboard was big enough. He pushed his back against the wall and stood still. The voices grew closer as the killers entered the room. They spoke in Tamil. Tau knew only a few words of the language.

"... bunch of idiots," one said. Tau couldn't see which.

"... shame... ...busy," the other replied. "...have them..."

"... later... ...what happens..."

Tau held his breath. His thoughts became jumbled.

Leo and Allissa assumed these men had been paid to kill them. Was that all?

The talking stopped. One of the waiters scrabbled around with dishes, and the door opened again. The other appeared at the entrance to the storeroom. He stepped forward and turned toward the fridge.

Tau stood statuesque, barely concealed by the shadow. The waiter hadn't seen him yet.

The fridge door squeeked as the waiter pulled it open. The sound of a fan rattled into the room.

The moments passed.

The waiter lifted something from the fridge. His biceps strained beneath the weight.

Tau tried to push himself harder against the wall. The cold, damp bricks dug into his shoulders.

The waiter stepped backwards.

Beads of sweat ran from the waiter's brow in the humid kitchen.

The man lifted a large metal tray from the fridge. On top of the tray was a slab of meat. It was thick, pink and fresh, with an exposed bone. The waiter removed the entire tray, then turned to face Tau.

Tau's jaw dropped, his eyes widened and he inhaled sharply.

The spell was broken. The waiter looked at Tau.

Tau didn't notice. He was looking at the cut of meat on the large metal tray. More specifically, Tau was looking at what was on the end of the cut of meat the waiter removed from the fridge.

Tau blinked, not quite believing what he saw.

On the end of the cut of meat, its skin pale from the cool of the refrigerator, was a human hand.

79

Tau tore his eyes from the hand and looked at the waiter. Their eyes locked. The waiter's eyes were dark pools and on his face contorted into a rancid, oily smile.

Tau was the first to move.

He dropped the rucksack into the shadow beside the cupboard and launched himself at the waiter. He sprung with all the force and speed he could muster.

The waiter, with no hands free, took the force in his shoulder. He was off balance.

The plate dropped. It crashed to the floor, and the arm rolled limp against the wall.

The waiter stumbled backwards. Tau recovered his balance and prepared to continue the attack. He was now engaged. This needed to happen.

He pushed the waiter with both hands, slamming him back against a metal cabinet on the far wall. Jars of spices skittered across the shelves and smashed to the floor.

The waiter lashed at Tau with his fingers and fists as he

struggled to recover his balance. Metal pans clanged to the tiled floor.

Tau knew his time was limited. He could probably deal with one of the men, but if the other came into the kitchen he was done for. The fight would either be over in the next few seconds, or Tau was going to lose. And that meant his death.

Tau pulled one of the long metal dishes from the counter and swung it high. It had been prepared with onions, spices and meat, ready for the oven. Food scattered around the kitchen. Tau didn't notice the weight as adrenaline pounded.

Tau didn't hesitate. This man had killed Jack.

TAU'S first strike thumped against the waiter's forearm. The man yelped in pain as something in his arm cracked.

Tau raised the dish again. This time the waiter, distracted by the agony in his arm, didn't react quickly enough. Tau brought the dish down. It connected with the side of his neck. The force was hard. The shock rippled up Tau's arm and stung his shoulder. The waiter crumpled to the floor.

Tau knew he had to leave. Now.

Tau opened the kitchen door and stepped back into the restaurant. His knuckles whitened around the dish. The restaurant was as it had been two minutes before. To Tau, weeks could have passed.

Fuli stood as soon as she saw Tau. Her previous expression of nonchalance quickly replaced by one of concern.

The other waiter was taking orders in the far corner of the room. He glanced up and saw Tau leave the kitchen. He straightened up. He was taller than his brother. Much taller.

The customers continued to talk. The waiter wasn't listening. His eyes bored into Tau.

Tau tightened his grip around the tray.

The blonde-haired customer was still trying to explain his order and tapped the big waiter on the forearm. He slapped the man's arm away and crossed the restaurant.

The noise in the restaurant subsided as all eyes darted between the waiter and Tau.

Tau's gaze dashed towards Fuli. Their eyes met. This was about to get nasty.

Tau swallowed hard and raised the tray above his head, both hands gripping the hefty metal platter.

Fuli darted for the door. Her stool clattered to the floor.

Tau needed to get out. He needed to get past the waiter, who was now only two strides away. He raised the tray higher, hoping the threat would be enough.

A collective gasp echoed around the restaurant. All eyes watched the waiter and Tau. People pushed their chairs backwards to get out of the way.

Tau held the dish high. He had one shot. The timing needed to be right.

Calculating distance, speed and time, Tau brought the tray down with everything he could.

One swing, one gesture, one hit, Tau just hoped it would be enough.

The waiter lunged forward and grabbed the tray. His firm grip closed around the metal. The platter jarred to a stop. The waiter showed no pain as he pulled the serving dish away from Tau and threw it to the floor. It skidded harmlessly to the concrete.

Then, with his lips parted in a grin, the waiter pushed Tau backwards against the wall.

Tau fought back with a right hook. The waiter didn't move.

Tau tried again with a fist to the stomach, but again the waiter made no sign of pain.

The big man straightened up. His grin widened.

Entranced diners gaped at the scene.

The world shook as the waiter delivered a crippling elbow to the side of Tau's face.

And another.

Tau slumped against the wall and waited for the third.

80

Insects circled the hanging bulb and two pairs of eyes watched the restaurant's shady door. There were so many insects that the bulb now looked like a solid globe. Only under scrutiny could it be recognised as thousands of darting, twisting creatures.

What was going on in there? All Tau needed to do was drop the bag and get out. What was taking so —

Leo's breath caught as the door moved. It opened slowly at first but then sprang back as Fuli ran out into the night. She had the look of a wild animal running from a predator. Unpredictable, dangerous.

Allissa stepped out of the shadow to show Fuli where they stood. Fuli's eyes darted, but her legs didn't stop. She ran full pelt away from the restaurant and into the warren of passages.

Allissa paused on the precipice of a decision. She looked at Leo, then ran after Fuli.

Leo turned to face the restaurant. It was him, the bulb, the door, and somewhere behind that, the restaurant and Tau.

Leo took a hesitant step as doubts swarmed his mind. He couldn't do this. Who was he to think that he could do this?

His chest tightened, and he struggled for breath. He couldn't do this.

Leo leaned forward and rested on his knees. The air tasted thin and sickening.

He pulled the deepest breath he could and looked up at the bulb against the dark orange sky. He remembered something that Allissa said that afternoon.

When the time comes I'd trust you to do the right thing.

Leo straightened up. He was not one of the insects that darted around the bulb in the turbulent night. He could choose what to do. He could choose the right thing.

Leo stepped forward. He put a hand on the flaking paint of the gloomy door and pushed.

Inside was chaos. One of the waiters stood facing the far wall of the restaurant with his back to Leo. Around him, diners stared in silence, ignoring their food and beers.

Tau slumped against the wall. His arms hung limp at his sides. One eye was already bloody.

A dull thump reverberated around the restaurant as the waiter cracked an elbow across Tau's face. It wasn't the first one from the look of things.

I'd trust you to do the right thing.

One of the heavy dishes lay on the ground beside the door. Leo bent slowly and picked it up. He raised the dish between shaking hands and walked stealthily, silently toward the man.

The moment was his.

Leo focused on the waiter. The man who had tried to kill them. The man who had chased them through the night. The man who had killed Jack and now was beating Tau.

I'd trust you to do the right thing.

Leo clenched his teeth, narrowed his eyes and slammed the dish down on the back of the waiter's head.

A crack rolled around the restaurant. Leo's arms jarred in shock. The waiter crumped to the floor.

81

Looking from the rear window of a taxi, Allissa watched as the passage leading to the restaurant grew small. Thinking of Jack, and the countless other people who hadn't made it out of the city because of that place, she hoped the events of the night would put an end to it forever. When they were safe, she and Leo would need to track down Jack's family. The thought was a horrible one, but his family needed to know the truth.

A few short minutes earlier, Allissa had followed Fuli, running in a state of shock. Catching up with her and putting an arm across her shoulders to slow her run, Allissa spoke to her in soothing tones. Allissa knew Fuli wouldn't understand, but perhaps the soft sounds would transcend her panic. When Fuli turned, her eyes still wild and wet, Allissa hugged her, told her it would be okay and that she was safe. The hug seemed to last a long time. When Allissa looked up, she saw Leo and Tau coming towards them. Tau was bloodied, swollen and resting on Leo's shoulder.

Two minutes later they'd squeezed into a taxi.

As the taxi rumbled and shook, Tau told the others what

he'd seen in the kitchen. Leo and Allissa listened in silent shock. Fuli looked disinterested out the front window.

"They do what?" Leo asked, hearing the description of the arm in the fridge.

"We weren't a one-off?" Allissa said, the memory of the meal they'd eaten rolling in her stomach. The colour drained from Leo's face.

"Seems that way," Tau said. "Seems like they've been doing this a while. You should've seen it. It was disgusting. Like a piece of meat at the butchers, you know? How they hang the carcass of the —"

"Stop the car!" Leo shouted, opening the door before it had.

Leo jumped out, ran to the side of the road and emptied his stomach into a drainage channel. The thought of eating there, eating a person, made Allissa feel the same.

"I'm sure it wasn't Jack's," Tau said apologetically. "It was too big for that. He was too skinny."

Allissa glanced at Tau's swollen face and swallowed back her nausea.

"What do we do? We've got to do something about that," Leo said, getting back in the car a couple of minutes later.

"Stick with the plan," Tau said. "If we go to the police and tell them what we know they'll laugh us out of there. But once they've gone and seen it for themselves, they can draw their own conclusions."

Allissa remembered the officers' reaction the morning they'd woken up in the cell. They'd been laughed out of the station once. She was in no rush to repeat it.

"This has played right into our plan," Tau concluded. "The bag's there too, right back in the kitchen. All we have to do is get the police through the door. We just need the final piece,"— he looked at Fuli —"then we'll get out of here."

Allissa and Leo nodded. Allissa had been against leaving Kathmandu at first. She'd just started putting down roots and didn't want to move on yet. But she knew Fuli and Chimini would get on just fine without her.

"Don't forget to invite our friend along," Allissa said.

Tau drew out his phone and dialled the number from the card left in the hotel. It connected straight away. He spoke in Nepalese, repeated the message in English, then hung up.

"I wish I could be there to see this go down. I'd like to give that guy a bit of... you know." Tau threw a punch into the air.

"Looks like he already got the better of you," Allissa said.

The taxi stopped outside the police station. Leo looked at the grey concrete building with uncomfortable recognition.

Fuli got out of the car and Allissa followed. Allissa knew the story they'd asked Fuli to tell wasn't far from the painful truth. Allissa hugged Fuli and wished she knew the words to praise her courage.

"Thank you," was all she managed, holding Fuli at arm's length for a moment.

Fuli turned and walked up the steps as Allissa climbed back into the waiting taxi.

Fuli reached the top of the stairs and stepped inside as the taxi pulled away into the light evening traffic. As the taxi turned a corner and the police station drew out of sight, Allissa wished all her problems would be solved with a visit there. Then she too could stop running.

82

Tired tourists pulled themselves through the door advertised by the bare bulb as the night wore on. The journey was hard, but to someone travelling the world, the harder it is to find something, the better it is when you do.

Regaining consciousness on the floor of the kitchen, the smaller of the two brothers rubbed his neck where the dish had connected. Standing on shaky legs, he made his way toward the restaurant where a commotion of voices boomed.

"We've been robbed," he said, looking around to see his brother lying on the floor. He was just about conscious, although dazed and confused. "We will contact the police tomorrow, do not worry." He urged anxious diners back to their seats. Service needed to continue. They couldn't have this sort of attention.

He helped his brother to his feet, and they swayed together back into the kitchen.

The customers would forget. Those that didn't would put it down to one of those great travelling stories. The brothers would ask around for the man tomorrow. They knew people in the city. They would find him, and they would deal with him.

The larger of the two rubbed the swollen red mark on the back of his head. It was lucky that whoever hit him hadn't got the angle quite right.

83

Outside the Teku Guesthouse, Leo and Tau waited in the taxi as Allissa packed some belongings. They each hoped that after the call they'd made, Stockwell's man would be on the way to the restaurant. Even so, they were vigilant and watched every parked and passing car for any sign of an unwanted observer.

A car crawled passed. Its bright lights illuminated the road and the square. Leo and Tau watched it suspiciously. As the light faded back to the lurid orange of the city, Tau continued to explain to the taxi driver what they wanted to do. They would employ him for the next two days. That's how long it would take to get where they were going, and for him to drive back to the city. Everything would need to be top secret, they stressed. He couldn't tell anyone, not before, not after.

Leo thought he should feel some kind of shock after the events of the day. He'd never seen that sort of violence, let alone caused it. He replayed the moment he'd brought the tray down on the back of the waiters' head. He felt the cold metal in his sweating palms, the pressure of the object arcing through the air, the diners' intake of breath, and the waiter folding to the floor.

Allissa reappeared, crossing the square with a small backpack. She walked away from the guesthouse, her home, with nothing more than a look of nonchalance. It was as though this were just another journey, just another day where she had to drop everything and leave at a moment's notice. Leo couldn't help but admire her confidence.

The taxi driver helped Allissa slot her bag into the tiny space behind the rear seats. They still had to get Tau and Leo's bags to fit. It was going to be a squeeze.

Back at the hotel, Leo packed quickly. The same hands which had held the dish, which had felt the sickening vibration as it connected with the skull of the waiter, now folded and packed the few items he'd used since they'd been there.

"You did the right thing," Allissa said. "I knew you would. I'd have done the same."

"I can't stop thinking about it," Leo replied. "Feeling the jolt. I know it was the right thing to do, and I know he killed people. But... well, I don't want him to be dead."

"He won't be, I'm sure," Allissa said, turning from the window. In silhouette, Allissa's expression was neither a smile nor a frown. Their eyes connected until Leo looked down at his hands.

"I think my father underestimated you," Allissa said, reaching over and taking his hand.

Leo hadn't felt the warm touch of another person's hand in a long time. It fitted naturally in his.

He looked at Allissa.

Footsteps echoed from somewhere in the hotel. One voice called, and another answered. Time was moving on.

"We've got to go," Tau said, stepping into the room without knocking. "You got everything?"

Leo stuttered.

"Yeah, let's go," Allissa said, passing Leo and following Tau out of the room. At the door, she turned and looked back at Leo. She was smiling; Leo was sure of it. Or maybe it was just the night.

Leo stuffed the final t-shirt into the bag and lifted it onto his back. He stopped at the door and caught a glimpse of himself in the mirror. He looked different; his long and shaggy hair now blended into the baggy t-shirt. He even looked slightly tanned. He was starting to look like one of the travellers who pulsed through the city.

He switched off the light and made for the stairs.

Out in the street, the taxi driver loaded their bags into the boot of the tiny car. It must have been thirty years old, and with each bag, the suspension sagged further.

Leo and Allissa slid into the back seat, and Tau got in the front. Tau needed to make sure the driver took them to the right place. He'd already loaded the navigation on his phone and plugged it into the car's charging block. The journey to Pokhara was two hundred kilometres and would take them many hours.

Finally, getting the boot to catch the driver got in too. Tau spoke to him in Nepalese. The driver grinned and touched the head of a small elephant icon on the dashboard. He turned the ignition, and the car spluttered to life.

All were too absorbed to notice another car, fifty meters behind, light up and ease in behind them on the empty road.

84

Green always used local help as often as possible. When trying to find people, innate knowledge of a city was crucial. Although cities were laid out around solid objects like buildings, streets, bridges, rivers and mountains, people flowed through them in organic and unpredictable ways. For example, why someone would travel halfway across the city, just to have a meal in this particular backstreet restaurant, Green didn't understand. They'd passed numerous restaurants already, each offering similar food for travellers.

"Down there," said his guide, a short Nepalese man whose quick steps Green felt like he'd been following for a month.

"Where?" Green said, stopping and squinting into the darkness. "I don't see —"

"Look close," the guide replied. "You see the light? Hangs above the door."

"That's the restaurant?"

"Yes."

"Well come on then. Let's go and see if they're there."

"No. I am not going in there," the small man said. His white teeth gleamed in the darkness. "That is no good restaurant."

"We're only going to look. We ate an hour ago."

"No." The guide shifted his weight from one foot to the other. "Not good restaurant. You go."

Green glared. He didn't have time for this. He set off down the dark passageway toward the restaurant on his own.

It was just a restaurant, a restaurant like any other. Green had come all this way, so if the answer lay behind that door, he was going to go inside and find it. Green paused at the door and looked up at the bulb. It swayed imperceptibly on its wire, like tendons beneath the skin.

Green shook his head and walked inside.

The first thing Green noticed was the noise. Two dozen people ate, drank and talked loudly. The next thing he noticed was the wet heat of the cooking, rich spices, onions, garlic. Green carefully looked at each person in turn. None looked much like Allissa Stockwell. He moved further into the restaurant and looked again. The call said this is where she would be, but she wasn't here yet.

A waiter emerged from a door at the back of the room. He carried two large sizzling dishes to the table in the far corner.

Green caught his eye. He would ask if Allissa was in here. Green took out his phone to find Allissa's picture. As he was looking, the phone rang in his hands. Green answered but couldn't understand the words against the noise of the restaurant.

"Hold on," he said. "I'll go outside."

As the door closed behind him, Green listened again.

"I have seen them. They are leaving. They got into taxi with bags, looks like they are leaving town."

"Okay, follow them," Green said. "Do not lose them. I'll get in a taxi and catch up with you."

Green turned his back on the restaurant and ran as quickly as the debris-strewn alleyway would allow. The waiter might have information, but a hot lead took priority. He could come back if needed.

"Taxi. Quick as possible!" Green shouted ahead to his guide. The small man didn't hide his relief.

Hurrying back toward the main road, they passed a group of men coming the other way. The group didn't pause as they reached the crossroads. The leaders ran straight for the hanging bulb illuminating the dark door.

"Police! Don't move!" the leader shouted as he pushed into the restaurant. His colleagues entered behind him and fanned out to block any exit.

It would take the police a while to understand what was really going on in the restaurant. They'd soon find the bag Tau had dropped in the kitchen. And on the floor nearby, they'd find a human arm.

85

The road from Kathmandu to Pokhara is well-travelled but treacherous. The dusty surface snakes across mountains, down valleys and through forests. Many times it clings precariously to the side of cliffs with nothing to break the deadly fall.

Fortunately for Allissa, Tau and Leo, the road at night was quiet. Bloated trucks lay dormant in any available space, their windscreens covered to give the sleeping drivers some privacy. They would start their plodding journey again at first light.

It's unusual to make the journey at night. It's dangerous enough in the day with the unpredictable road and the perilous drops. But for Leo and the others, it was essential.

The city rolled past silently for the first half an hour. Dark windows had been closed to the outside world as hardworking residents got a few hour's rest. Eventually, the lights faded as the areas of darkness between them grew. Soon, the taxi's dim yellow headlights were alone in the night.

The driver dropped down a gear and accelerated toward

a hill. He was still driving as though they were swarming through the city. Tau reassured him that they didn't need to rush. At first the driver didn't seem to understand, then he laid off the pressure, sat back slightly and fell into a more sedentary pace. The engine even calmed from its usual scream of protest to a compliant, productive hum.

In the back, Leo and Allissa dozed. The lights of the city which had drawn their attention had been replaced by absolute darkness. Only the occasional lights of other cars pricked their eyes as they passed, inches from their own.

After an hour, the driver slowed as they pulled through a collection of houses. Tau, who himself was losing focus as the exhaustion of the day caught up on him, asked what was happening.

"Petrol," the driver said, tapping the gauge on the display which crept toward empty.

Leo awoke as the bright white light of the petrol station flooded into the car. They pulled alongside two white painted pumps. Their analogue dials showed a row of zeros. Two garlands of yellow flowers hung in the still air.

The driver got out and walked across the forecourt to a small cabin, where he spoke to a man through an open window. Switching on the pump looked like more of a complex transaction than it might be in Europe.

Tau took the opportunity to stretch.

Leo followed. It felt good to be out. He pushed his arms skyward and straightened his legs. Allissa did the same, rubbing her eyes.

The cool, fresh night air was welcome. The smell was different here. The jungle and the humid night mingled with the spice of local cooking and burning incense. Leo's muscles relaxed and his mind calmed.

Leo stretched again, tilting his head backwards and

pushing his shoulder blades together while looking at the sky. Gone was the orange glow of Kathmandu. Here the sky was black; the darkest, purest black Leo had seen in a long time. Between the clear expanses of black, stars peppered the sky. In Brighton, only if you looked closely, you could see a dozen or so stars whose bullish light seeped through the clouds. But here you could see stars between stars, stars circling stars in great swathes of brilliance. It occurred to Leo that they were always there, like a universe of possibilities, only sometimes they couldn't be seen. He supposed in those times you just had to believe that they were there. You had to believe that the night sky wasn't just a few bright lights, but thousands of them, each in a cycle of resurrection and decay.

A car drove into the petrol station behind their taxi. Its harsh lights cast long shadows, scanning the jungle, the cabin, and dazzling Leo. The engine stuttered to a halt, and the lights died. The silence thickened.

Leo didn't think anything of it until he saw Tau tense. The car was the same as the one they were travelling in — another taxi from Kathmandu. Not unusual in the city where the roads teemed with them, but less common this far away.

"Allissa Stockwell?" came a voice from the darkness — a man's voice.

Leo, Tau and Allissa looked at each other.

Their driver was still talking at the window. The petrol station canopy was an island of light, surrounded by impenetrable darkness. There was nowhere to go. The trio stood silent and motionless.

A man climbed from the back seat of the small car. His face was still hidden in shadow.

"Are you Allissa Stockwell?" he asked again, stepping into the light.

He wasn't the sort of person Leo expected to be doing Stockwell's dirty work. Slight, short, with an intelligent gaze and light hair. He was well dressed, an unusual quality for Europeans in Nepal.

No one answered.

Tau was at the back, Allissa in the middle. Leo was nearest.

"I'm sorry, let me introduce myself," said the man, sensing the group's apprehension. "I'm Marcus Green. I'm a journalist." He looked directly at Allissa. "I'm currently investigating your dad for fraud, extortion and blackmail. I know about your mother. I would like to talk to you. I imagine you've got a lot you could say."

Leo and Allissa exchanged glances. No one moved.

"How can we trust you?" Leo asked. If the last few days had taught them anything, it was that they had to keep their guard up until they were sure.

"I have ID," Green said, passing Leo a leather wallet. "But that only tells you who I am. You're going to have to decide yourselves whether to trust me or not."

Leo flicked the wallet open. Inside was a yellow and blue press card in the place where people often kept photos of their families. Leo flicked through the other cards. All of them corroborated his name. Leo passed the wallet back.

"Lift your shirt up," Tau said. "Show us you haven't got a weapon."

"Seriously?" Green said, glancing from face to face. Seeing no retraction, he lifted his shirt and showed his pale, slim stomach. "Can we talk now?"

Leo and Tau nodded.

Green explained how he'd first heard of Stockwell when

investigating MPs misusing their expenses. With a little bit of digging, he told them, he found there to be a lot more going on than just a few bogus claims.

"There was a case of bribery within the party, the blackmail of a local business owner, and some unsavoury investments," he said. "But that's not all. Stockwell used a phone box to make calls he didn't want traced. He's old school like that. We managed to, uh, overhear a few of those calls. In one of them, he talked about you." The register of Green's voice dropped. His eyes locked on Allissa. "He discussed 'dealing with you'. At first, I thought I was jumping to conclusions. But when I heard the recording myself, there was no other option."

Leo looked from Green to Allissa, waiting for a reaction. There was none.

"Of course, we were worried about you. People go missing all the time. Without the call, it would've been impossible to trace a link. That's partly why I'm here, to make sure you're safe."

A motorbike rattled past, its engine sinking back into the noise of the jungle.

"This story is going to be published next week. I'll hand my research over to the police. I want the story to be as full as possible, so I needed to talk to you first." Allissa said nothing. "There will most likely be charges brought against your father for this. For his financial misdealings, for what I just told you, and something else which I'm not sure you'll know."

Their taxi driver returned from his negotiation and started to fill the car with fuel. Green's driver was now talking to the man in the petrol station. Leo wondered whether they had any idea what was going on.

The driver squeezed the nozzle. The pump shuddered to

life, protesting against the arduous task with a series of knocks and bangs. The canopy's lights dimmed and flickered with the strain on the electric current.

The four moved away to the back of Green's taxi.

"First, if it's okay with you," Green said to Allissa, "I'd like to ask you a couple of questions. Just to check I've got the full story. Then you can ask me anything you want to know. I wouldn't want you to be surprised by anything you read in the newspaper."

"I'll tell you what I know," Allissa said, angling a challenging stare at Green.

The knocking from the pump trailed to a stop, and the lights bounced back. Tau explained to the taxi driver that they needed a few more minutes to talk to the man. The driver nodded and ambled back toward the cabin.

The four moved back into the light and Green placed the phone on the roof of the taxi. He started recording.

Without preamble, Allissa told her story, every painstaking detail of it. She was calmer this time, more detached from the moment her family was torn apart by stratospheric lies. It were as though she had started to leave the past where it was. Green asked a couple of questions. He was doing a good job, Leo admitted, giving Allissa the freedom to speak and prompting for details when needed.

The taxi driver brought them four cups of sweet-smelling chai.

Allissa continued until she'd relayed every detail. Lie by lie, blow by blow.

"Thank you," Green said, picking up and switching off the phone. "I realise that wasn't easy. Particularly against your father. But he really is an evil man."

Allissa nodded.

"There is something I need to tell you, something you

don't yet know," Green said. "The real reason your father would go to such lengths to keep you from coming back."

"What?" Allissa said, her eyes emotionless, detached.

"We noticed some time ago that Stockwell was making rather large monthly payments to a person we didn't know. We couldn't work out why. Then the vault of a private bank in Brighton was broken into, and the payments stopped. We figured —"

"Get to it," Allissa said. "What do you know?"

"I think I know what was in that box, although as yet I can't prove it." Green's voice became even deeper. "Allissa, it concerns your mother. Her death wasn't an accident."

86

"I don't think I've ever been anywhere as beautiful as this," Leo says as the colour drains from the sky and the noise of the island swells. Birds flash through the twilight streaks of pink and purple.

"I knew you'd like it," Mya replies in a whisper, her feet kicking the water which laps beneath the jetty.

"How did we get here? I mean, this is crazy, like it's a different world," Leo says, pointing towards the inky ocean in front of them. They've been travelling for two months, but this is the first time they've seen an ocean like this.

A bird squawks and the light of a boat creeps across the horizon.

"Koh Tao is a special place because it's hard to get to. When things are hard to find, that's when they're precious." Mya looks out into nothing. Her hands grip the side of the jetty and her feet swing freely. She's beautiful. Her smile is currency across the world.

"I'm just glad to be here... with you," Leo says, looking at her profile in the light of the setting sun. "Even the extra month. I'm so happy to be here."

This is the time, he knows it, tonight. He's had the ring hidden in his wallet for over a month now, waiting for tonight. This time, this place, this woman.

Mya turns to face Leo as he lies back on the jetty. Water slaps the supports beneath the platform. Somewhere nearby, people speak in an unfathomable language.

"I knew you'd like it," Mya says.

"Yeah, I'm struggling to take it in, I've never been anywhere as beautiful as this," Leo says, resting up on his elbows.

Now would be the perfect moment.

Mya leans forward.

"To be... to be here with you is so special," Leo says as Mya turns to look at him. "And we... I mean, I hadn't even planned to come here."

"Yeah, it's been great," Mya says, turning back to the water. A chill passes across her body, blowing her loose-fitting top tight against her profile. Leo's eyes follow; he can't help it.

He turns and fumbles the ring from his wallet. The one-kneed stance that tradition dictates isn't possible on the jetty, but Leo hopes the setting and moment will make up for it.

This needs to be perfect. It will be perfect.

Leo takes a deep breath, the sea air, the smell of tamarind, lime, of love, hope and opportunity.

Then he exhales.

"Will you marry me?"

An eddy of wind skips past, rushing towards the curving palm trees on the shoreline. The bay shivers. Time hangs in the balance. Leo holds his breath, unblinking.

"I..." Mya stalls, following a train of thought but cutting it before it starts. She looks from Leo's expectant expression to the ring in his hands. "Oh my gosh, that's so beautiful." She plucks it from his fingers.

Mya holds up the ring. Its colours refract in the twilight.

"Come to our room in five minutes," she says, climbing to her feet. "Then you'll get your answer."

Mya stands, turns and walks toward the beach.

Leo settles back on his elbows, stares at the bruised horizon, and tries to ignore the bitter sting of disappointment.

That's so typical of Mya, doing things her way.

87

They always just seemed so normal.

While listening to Green speak, Allissa thought of those TV interviews in which surprised neighbours describe how shocked they are that the person next door has done something terrible.

It's so unexpected.

Not for her. It wasn't like that at all for Allissa. Somehow, she knew exactly what Green was going to say.

"Your father paid a group of people in Kenya to kill your mother and make it look like an accident. To make it look like she was caught up in a protest. Your father thought he had got away with it."

Allissa could picture it all. Chubby fingers dialling the call. Rolls of flesh wobbling as instructions were given. Sweaty brow wiped ceremoniously after hanging up the phone. Her only disappointment was that she hadn't worked it out for herself.

"Then there was a regime change in Kenya," Green continued, "and one of the men he'd hired liked the idea of living all expenses paid in the U.K. With the evidence he had about what your father had done, he pretty much got away with it."

What surprised Allissa the most, listening to Green beneath the swathes of shimmering stars, was that she still didn't feel anything. She thought that maybe she should feel shocked, or horrified, or scared, or surprised, or useless. But she just felt nothing. She felt empty.

Climbing back into the taxi a few minutes later, Allissa wished she could feel something. But she didn't. She just didn't.

With the squeal of engines and the crunch of tyres, the two taxis headed opposite ways down the narrow strip of tarmac. Green had turned west back toward Kathmandu, where he planned to get on the first flight back to London. Allissa, Leo and Tau pushed on east toward Pokhara.

It wasn't until the taxi started to wallow through the darkness that Allissa began to feel something. It wasn't shock or horror. All she felt was relief. Pure relief.

She now wasn't the only one who knew her father's true nature. At least one other person, the journalist now heading the other way, who knew what he had done . Soon he would publicise it to millions.

Would that free her from carrying his secrets everywhere she went? Allissa didn't know. But as the road stretched out, all boundless and bare, she felt a positivity that her freedom was out there somewhere.

After a few minutes of driving through the insipid darkness, the driver began speaking to Tau. He spoke in Nepalese, but made an effort to use the English words he knew.

Allissa and Leo listened intently.

Leo heard the word "home" used several times.

Tau turned to translate.

"Horan — he indicated to the taxi driver by name — "says his family home is nearby, ten minutes farther down this road. He suggests that we stop for a few hours and get some rest. They'll have food, and somewhere we can sleep. We'll continue tomorrow."

There was no reason not to. The road had been empty since they'd left the petrol station and all were tired. Leo and Allissa nodded.

A few minutes later, they turned off the main road and started up a thin farm track. Horan stopped the taxi and killed the engine. There was no sound, other the murmur of insects and the whisper of wind through the trees.

Horan asked them to follow him.

"This is where his family lives," Tau translated.

The darkness was faultless. As Allissa's eyes got used to it, she saw the outlines of trees against the ocean of stars. Horan walked up the hill, avoiding plants, trees and uneven ground. The others followed his quick footsteps.

They reached a back building, and Horan pushed open the door. Instinctively, he found a switch and warm light swamped them.

The room was comfortable. A light dampened by a wicker shade hung in the middle, and three wicker chairs surrounded a table.

Horan shouted a greeting. A young woman appeared from a door at the back, squinting against the light. Her face brightened when she saw Horan, and she rushed across the room to greet him. She looped her arms around his thin neck and pulled him close. When she noticed the others, she straightened her posture and smiled. An older man and woman followed from a different door wearing the same bleary expressions. They too brightened as they welcomed

Horan home. Horan introduced them one by one and Tau translated for Leo and Allissa.

"This is Horan's mother, father and wife. He says we should sit. He will find us something to drink and eat."

Allissa felt like an intruder. They were real family, working together, supporting each other. Horan's wife woke the children and brought them from the bedroom to see their father. They rubbed their eyes with limp hands and beamed at their daddy.

"These taxi drivers work so hard. Horan hasn't seen his family for a month. You have given him this great opportunity to see them tonight," Tau said.

Horan's father offered Allissa the chair, but she refused. Horan's wife brought a pile of cushions from a bedroom and Allissa stacked them against one of the walls. Leo and Allissa sat together and listened to happy conversation they didn't understand. Tau sat on the opposite side of the room, shouting across some translations.

No one had slept enough in the last few days. They'd been constantly on edge, guessing and worrying about what was coming next. Right here, listening to the family whose brief unity they had caused, Allissa felt the tight coils of pressure start to slowly unwind.

Through heavy eyes, Allissa glanced from one person to the next. Some she'd just met, some she'd known for just a few days, but in the warmth of their company, she felt more comfortable than she had for a long time.

Maybe home isn't a place, she thought, resting her head on Leo's shoulder. *Maybe it's a feeling.*

88

Five minutes must be up, Leo thinks, turning his back on the Koh Tao night. The sea curls up behind him, and the stars lead anywhere he could want to go. Tonight, however, he doesn't want to be anywhere but here.

Koh Tao is beautiful, and to arrive with Mya is one of the most completing experiences of his life.

The perfect place, he thinks, remembering the warm shape of the ring in his palm.

The sound of the island intensifies around him. Two animals yammer somewhere far off. Sea and sand breathe together in harmony, and insects call to one another in the undergrowth.

Light from the window of the cabin they're staying in shimmers across the water.

Somewhere up the road, a car starts. Its engine whines for a moment before fading.

Leo reaches the cabin and looks back out across the dark ocean. Above him, the map of stars spreads back to his flat in Brighton. That life feels so far away, but to which they will return. In this moment, though, on this beautiful island, waiting for the answer to the question of his life, it feels like a world away.

"I'm coming in," Leo says to the door.

He braces himself and pulls it open. The room is how they left it. Bags, clothes, the made up bed, the long mirror.

Where's Mya?

She must be in the bathroom.

He moves over to the door.

"Hey, you're full of surprises tonight."

Nothing. The world is silent.

"I'm coming in."

He turns the handle. The door moves.

White tiles.

Shower.

He holds his breath.

Sink.

His chest tightens.

Mirror.

Towels folded over the rail, the shower unused.

The bathroom's empty.

No Mya.

89

Dawn broke over the valley like it had every morning for fifty million years. Starting low, it lit a line between the uppermost mountain ridges and the sky. At first, a thin fracture in the darkness, growing bigger with each moment until the tops of the mountains flared. It then moved on to the lower slopes, lighting each in order, the way an artist might paint a canvas.

Leo stood outside Horan's family home, looking across the tumbling landscape to the white peaks, behind which the sun prepared to rise.

Sunrise is celebrated the world over for its beauty, its simplicity and its inherent hope; this was the most hopeful sunrise Leo had seen in a long time.

Kathmandu and its slovenly passageways, hidden restaurants, noise and dust, all seemed like a different planet entirely.

"It's amazing what a bit of sleep can do," Allissa said, joining him and rubbing her eyes.

Her hair stood up on one side where she'd slept on his shoulder. He smiled as their elbows touched.

"This is not a bad place to wake up," Leo said.

"It's beautiful, isn't it?"

The morning had a cold, fresh bite.

"I think I could wake up here every morning and never get bored," Allissa said as a slither of sun appeared over the mountains.

Leo didn't reply. He was captivated by the scene.

A large bird pounded the still air.

The morning was fresh and innocent, but the day was coming. With each inch of the rising sun, the temperature would grow, people would wake, and traffic would rumble.

Voices came from the house. They spoke quickly, excitedly, until from outside they couldn't be distinguished from each other. The door opened, and Tau stepped out, he too rubbing the night from his dark eyes.

"They're making us breakfast," he said. "Sleep alright?"

Leo and Allissa nodded and followed Tau inside.

Colourful plates and cups filled with a vegetable soup, roti and milky sweet chai covered the table. It wasn't until Leo started to eat that he realised how hungry he was. The others felt the same and ate ravenously. Horan's mother refilled their bowls, and his wife brought more bread from the kitchen.

When they'd eaten all they could, Horan, Tau, Leo and Allissa made their way back to the taxi. The friends received hugs and smiles from all members of Horan's family. Leo forced Horan's father to take some money for their hospitality. Although he initially refused, Tau's encouragement eventually wore him down.

Leo slid into the taxi and longed for a shower. That was the first thing he'd do when they arrived in Pokhara. Horan started the engine, and they started down the track with Horan's family waving them goodbye.

The main road thronged with traffic. Cars, lorries and buses drooled past, bumper to bumper on the thin, precarious pot-holed tarmac.

Leo glanced nervously at the river hundreds of feet below the mountain road. If Horan was to slip, or one of the oncoming vehicles were to misjudge, the tiny car wouldn't stand a chance. He tried not to think of it and lay back, letting the wallowing vibrations of the car relax him.

Six hours later, in the heat of the midday sun, they drove into Pokhara.

The car crawled down a lakeside road surrounded by luscious, green, forest-covered hills. Pagodas stood out above the trees in glistening white and gold. Restaurants spilled onto wide pavements. Tourists sauntered beside the water.

"Right here," Tau said, directing them to a hotel.

They pulled up outside a white-painted building and got out of the car. Leo stretched his muscles back into use.

They'd offered Horan a night in the hotel, thinking he wouldn't want to make the return journey straight away, but he refused. Unloading their bags and pocketing the money and tip, Horan was back in the car in less than three minutes. Leo suspected he would use the extra money to spend a few days with his family in their beautiful house. He deserved it.

Tau checked them into their rooms on the top floor overlooking the lake. They each dragged their bags upstairs. Leo and Allissa were sharing a twin room, and Tau was next door. Leo and Allissa hadn't discussed sharing, but when the receptionist said that was all they had available, neither seemed to mind. Secretly, the thought of having company was welcomed by both.

Tau suggested they meet later for food — there were

many good restaurants and bars in Pokhara, and they deserved a drink or three.

Leo and Allissa stumbled into the room and dropped their bags. Allissa lay on the bed nearest the door and Leo started the shower. Neither spoke.

While the shower ran hot, Leo charged his phone. It had died sometime in the last twenty-four hours without him even noticing. He planned to block and delete Stockwell's number as soon as the phone powered on.

As steam began to emanate from the bathroom door, Leo got up, undressed and stepped beneath the jets, letting the water rinse away the stresses of the week. It enlivened and invigorated his senses. He washed quickly, then just stood there with the water running over him.

The last few days were a blur. Leo's phone beeped several times from the bedroom. He ignored it.

Finally, he shut off the water, dried off, wrapped himself in a towel and padded back into the bedroom.

From the window, the blue surface of the lake skipped and shuddered in the early afternoon light. Beyond, the pine-covered hills sparkled through a revitalising haze.

Leo looked at Allissa's sleeping figure. She had brought him here. Her tragedy, her grief, had now become twisted with his. Circumstances had muddled their lives without control.

Allissa turned in her sleep, her dark hair fanning across the pillow behind her.

Leo's phone beeped again. He picked it up from the pillow behind him and collapsed backwards. One text message was from his mum, one from his sister, and one from his Nepalese network provider. Another was from Stockwell.

Leo wasn't sure why — maybe it was the thought of

having won the game causing a boastful streak — but he looked at Stockwell's message first. Then he would delete it and block the number.

It was typically concise:

You have information I want, but I also have information you want. I'll tell you everything I know if you tell me where my daughter is.

It took Leo a few moments to see the attached picture.

His heart beat through his throat, and he jerked upright. His stomach made a fist.

He had to see this.

He tapped on the icon, and an image filled the screen. It was a face he hadn't seen for over two years. The dark hair tied high, strong cheekbones, broad smile, big eyes. And behind her, the unmistakable landscape of somewhere Leo knew she wanted to visit. Hong Kong.

EPILOGUE

Faith and Zain sat on the platform of Paddington Station. It had been a busy day, and Zain was tired. They'd caught the train from their home in Reading this morning for an appointment at the passport office. Zain was five, and Faith, his mother, wanted a passport for the country she'd lived in for nearly fifteen years. It was an expensive process and had taken her years of saving to accrue the necessary money even to complete the application. She'd taken the day off work too, but it would all be worth it when Zain was settled in the place he knew as home.

The train slid into the platform and a handful of people tumbled out. It was quiet coming into London, but it would be busy going the other way. People waited, most reading on their phones, some looking into nothing, all ignoring each other. As the train stopped they surged forward. Faith couldn't keep up with Zain holding her hand. They watched the crowd pass. They would wait. There would be enough space for all of them.

They walked to the far end of the platform where it

seemed less busy and got on the train. It was quiet here, and they both found seats. Zain closed his eyes on the manic city. It had been his first time in London. Faith wished she could have made it special, shown him the places they only knew from pictures. She hadn't been to the capital for at least ten years, rarely escaping the cycle of work and family commitments.

The carriage was almost empty. Only one other traveller, a large man, sat at the far end of the car.

As he tried to find comfort in the seat, Stockwell glanced around. The first class carriage of the train was almost empty. He hated getting the train. The whole thought of it made his skin itch. A place where people all travelled together. All sorts of people.

But this afternoon he wasn't just getting the train home. If that were the case, he'd have brought the Bentley. This afternoon he was on the train to meet someone. A man. A man who Stockwell hoped would put an end to a problem that had plagued him for years.

Exhaling, Stockwell pulled his briefcase from the floor and clicked it open. He removed a newspaper and then glanced at the contents of the case. A few sheets of old paper made it look less suspicious. Looking left and then right, he slid his fingers into the compartment on the lid and felt the thick bundle of notes hidden inside. He'd have paid ten times this for the freedom that would soon be his.

Stockwell locked the case and returned it to the floor. It would all be over — he checked his watch — in thirty minutes.

He spread his copy of the Financial Times across the table and slouched back into the seat. Thirty minutes. No time at all. It was actually yesterday's newspaper, and he knew most of the stories, but that didn't matter. He wasn't going to read it. He only had it because he needed something so they would recognize him.

He shuffled the paper and turned the page mechanically. The words squirmed in front of his eyes. It had been a frustrating day. Although he was mostly retired from political life, he still went into the House of Lords when the socialists were trying to sneak something through. Today had been one such occasion. They were voting on a bill to give disabled people the money they needed to make their lives as comfortable as possible.

Stockwell shook his head at the thought. It was likely to cost millions, billions even.

Why are people in this government hell-bent on bankrupting the country?

The doors hissed closed, and the train slid slowly from the platform. It rocked across the sixteen lines leading out of the station, then settled into the tracks towards Reading. Stockwell couldn't wait to get there and drive the Bentley the rest of the way home.

He looked around the carriage anxiously. His contact was supposed to meet him here. That had been the arrangement. Stockwell suddenly felt exposed; his contact knew what he looked like, but Stockwell had no idea who would be making the drop-off.

His hands tightened on the tabletop as he scanned the other seats. Besides the woman and her child, the place was empty. Stockwell turned to look at the seats behind him. They were empty too. The first class section was quiet. The hum of the standard class section emanated from through the sliding glass doors. Stockwell checked his watch and grimaced.

He turned back to face the quiet first class section and found himself looking at his only fellow traveller. The lady at the other end of the carriage. She was pretty. Her contented smile as the city passed city contrasted her dark skin. A small boy slept against her arm. Strangely, she reminded him of the woman who had brought him all this trouble in the first place. The woman who had fought and fought and fought, and in the end had to be silenced. Stockwell felt a surge of anger spark through him. The fact this was still haunting him after all these years was incredibly frustrating. She was the one who had created these issues. She had chosen her path. Although, he had always known the world wouldn't see it that way. That's why he had to silence things. Make it stop.

Today, he thought, turning the page of the paper again, that would finally be over.

But, the woman on the train was attractive. There was no disputing that. Stockwell leaned back into the seat. The way the light patterned across her face, her quick eyes taking in the outside world, her baggy jumper hugging across her chest. At this last observation, he crossed his legs.

He felt his face contort into something of a smile. The smile didn't last long.

"I have what you need," rumbled a deep voice from behind him.

Stockwell began to look round.

"Do not turn," the voice hissed. "Eyes forward."

A man in a long coat knelt to tie a shoelace in the aisle. The man placed another briefcase next to Stockwell's.

The man stood and lifted Stockwell's matching briefcase instead.

"Do not open it until after the next station," the man said, straightening up.

Without taking his eyes from the newspaper, Stockwell nodded.

"And this is the only copy?" Stockwell asked through clenched teeth.

"Of course," the man said. "That was the deal."

A computerized voice told passengers they were arriving at Slough.

The train began to slow, and the man took a step backwards and out of Stockwell's view. The whole exchange had taken less than ninety-seconds. Stockwell kept his eyes fixed on the newspaper as the train ground to a halt and the doors slid open. He pulled the briefcase in close to his leg. Inside was his freedom, emancipation from a man who'd kept him trapped for far too long.

As the train pulled away from Slough, Stockwell felt his mood lighten. It was done.

There's no rush now, Stockwell thought, peering out at the houses lining the track. The terrace, built in a uniform style over a century ago, had now distorted into a jumble of random-looking buildings. Some had boxy roof extensions; others had open areas with big-leaved plants. Stockwell moved his tongue around his teeth and closed his fingers around the briefcase's handle.

He folded the newspaper and placed the briefcase on the table in front of him. He unclipped the latches, cracked open the lid an inch, and looked around. The woman still gazed out at the city while her son continued to sleep. Stockwell rubbed his hand across his mouth.

He pulled open the briefcase and looked inside. An unmarked yellow folder was the only thing within. Stockwell picked it up and flipped open the lid. As his eyes rested on the contents, a self-satisfied smile broke across his reddened face.

"WHAT'RE you going to do now?" Leo asked Allissa as they turned their backs on the white dome of the World Peace Pagoda and looked out across Pokhara. A jumble of colourful buildings fought for space between the luscious, forest-covered hills and blueish green lakes. In the distance, the towering Annapurna ridges glimmered. Leo held the railing and felt the view shimmer in front of his eyes. It was too much to take in. Too beautiful.

"Probably just walk back down there and get some lunch," Allissa said, pointing down at the row of restaurants on the lake's shore.

They'd spent the last three days walking between places to eat and drink. Although neither could even begin to forget the haunting horror of Kathmandu, at least here it seemed a long way away.

"That's not really what I meant," Leo said, pulling a lungful of the thick hot air. He felt out of shape. The hike up the hill had taken them nearly two hours in the sweltering heat.

"What're you going to do when we leave here?"

"Oh, right," Allissa said. "I'm not sure. Hadn't thought about it. Go back to Kathmandu, I suppose." Her hands gripped the railing more firmly at the thought.

The lake shivered. Leo looked at the people strolling on the wide pavements in the distance.

"I mean, I've not got any plans, but with Tau heading off yesterday I thought you'd be wanting to go soon too," Leo said. Before leaving, Tau had arranged for them to have their twin room in the hotel for as long as they needed it. Last night had been their first night alone together. Leo and Allissa had walked along the lake, eaten a vegetarian curry in a quiet restaurant, enjoyed a couple of beers in one of the tourist bars, then fallen asleep in their twin beds.

"I don't know," Allissa said absently.

A group of tourists behind them whooped for a photograph.

Leo frowned. *I could just ask her, couldn't I?*

His mouth formed the shape of the words, but no sound came out. He watched the paragliders skipping through the air above the opposite peak.

"You could..." he started, stopping again as he heard the words stumble out.

"What?"

"You could come back to Brighton —"

Leo's voice was interrupted by a shrill noise from Allissa's pocket.

"How's anyone calling me?" she grumbled. "No one has this number." She pulled out her phone. "It's that journalist, Green." She prodded the screen. "Hello..."

Two minutes later, Allissa hung up the phone and turned to face Leo. Her eyes were wide and absent.

"It's my dad," Allissa said.

———

STOCKWELL'S SMILE didn't diminish for a moment in the final fifteen minutes of the train journey. As the train approached Reading station, he carefully folded the paper and dropped it back into the briefcase. Stockwell now had to decide whether to put the documents somewhere no one would ever find them, or eradicate them completely. Ultimately, he knew he should destroy them. Then they could never incriminate him again. But, seeing them had given him such a thrill. It felt like winning. And Stockwell loved winning.

As the train pulled to a stop, Stockwell stood, fastened

his jacket and picked up the briefcase. The woman with her son was also gathering her things. Stockwell waited for her to step out in front of him. As his eyes passed across her body, he felt a shudder of excitement.

"Thank you," she whispered, trying not to wake the boy whose head rested on her shoulder. Her voice was sharp and accented. Stockwell liked it incredibly.

"You're welcome," he boomed, patting down his suit.

Stockwell made his way through the station and out to the car park. He'd parked the Bentley in a quiet corner across two spaces. He did have further to walk, but it was worth it because it stopped idiots parking next to him.

He turned the corner, and the Bentley came into view. The station's hubbub of voices had faded now. The train murmured as it accelerated away from the station. Stockwell looked at his car and scowled. Some prick in a blue BMW had parked right next to him. The whole point of parking this far away was —

"Lord Stockwell." He didn't have time to finish the thought. "I'm writing an article about your dealings with a known Kenyan murderer. Have you got anything you'd like to say before it's published tomorrow?"

Stockwell saw the man step out from beside the BMW. The Lord's lips knitted and his brow darkened. "Absolutely nothing to say." Stockwell unlocked the Bentley and stepped towards the door.

"Are you sure? It could be the last opportunity to get your point heard while you're a free man?"

Stockwell turned and prepared to threaten the man with his usual legal action. Then he stopped. From the street, he heard the wail of sirens drawing near.

Hong Kong

Leo and Allissa's next case takes them to Hong Kong.
You can read it now:

www.lukerichardsonauthor.com/hongkong

"If you're missing travel at the moment and love a good thriller, I would definitely recommend this series."

"Exceptional piece of work."

"What a fabulous follow up!"

"Another fantastic book from Luke Richardson, it had me gripped from page one."

"An excellent and original story which will stay with you."

Hong Kong

When Jamie's colleague and former lover goes missing, the police start to ask questions. After a panicked call comes to light and traces of blood are discovered in his car, the net closes in. Sure, a body hasn't been found, but there's plenty of evidence to land Jamie behind bars.

Back from Kathmandu and working together to find missing people, Leo and Allissa take the case. All they have to do is find a woman who's supposed to be dead, to free a man charged with murder. But, when the investigation leads to the backstreets and building sites of Hong Kong, things get more difficult than either had imagined.

As predator becomes prey and lives become expendable, Leo and Allissa must face one of the city's most dangerous men, as well as battling ghosts from their own past.

With a man's freedom hanging in the balance and their relationship under strain, can they find what they're looking for before it's too late?

HONG KONG is the second of Luke Richardson's international thriller series. If you like fast-paced mysteries, you'll love this compulsive sequel.

Pick up HONG KONG to continue this series today!

www.lukerichardsonauthor.com/hongkong

WHAT HAPPENED IN KOH TAO?

Read the series prequel novella for free now:
www.lukerichardsonauthor.com/kohtao

"Intense, thrilling, mysterious and captivating."

"The story grabs you, you're on the boat with your stomach pitching. As the story gathers pace the tension is palpable. It's a page turner which keeps you hooked until the final word."

The evocative writing takes you to a place of white sand, the turquoise sea and tranquilly. But on an island of injustice and exploitation, tranquillity is the last thing Leo finds."

"Love and adventure collide in Thailand, love it!"

KOH TAO

Leo's looking for the perfect place to propose to the love of his life. When they arrive in the Thai tropical paradise of Koh Tao, he thinks he's found it.

But before he gets an answer, she's nowhere to be seen.

On searching the resort, his tranquillity turns to turmoil. Is it a practical joke? Has she run away? Or is it something much more sinister?

Set two years before Luke Richardson's international thriller series, this compulsive novella turns back the clock on an anxiety ridden man battling powerful forces in a foreign land.

KOH TAO is the prequel novella to Luke Richardson's international thriller series. Grab your copy for free and find out where it all began!

www.lukerichardsonauthor.com/kohtao

This book is dedicated to all those I've travelled beside.
First, foremost and always, Mark and Valerie, Mum and Dad.
Your sense of courage and adventure is my inspiration.

JOIN MY MAILING LIST

During the years it took me to write plan and this book, I always looked to its publication as being the end of the process. The book would be out, and the story would be finished.

Since releasing it in May 2019, I realised that putting the book into the world was actually just the start. Now I go on the adventure with every conversation I have about it. It's so good to hear people's frustrations with Leo's reserve, their shock at the truth about the grizzly backstreet restaurant, and their questions about what's going to happen next.

Most of these conversations happen with people on my mailing list, and I'd love you to join too.

I send an email a couple of times a month in which I talk about my new releases, my inspirations and my travels.

Sign up now:

www.lukerichardsonauthor.com/mailinglist

OTHER BOOKS BY LUKE RICHARDSON

Leo & Allissa International Thrillers

Koh Tao

www.lukerichardsonauthor.com/kohtao

Kathmandu

www.lukerichardsonauthor.com/kathmandu

Hong Kong

www.lukerichardsonauthor.com/hongkong

Berlin

www.lukerichardsonauthor.com/berlin

New York

www.lukerichardsonauthor.com/newyork

Riga

www.lukerichardsonauthor.com/riga

The Liberator: Kayla Stone Vigilante Thrillers

Justice is her beat

Her name is Kayla Stone

She is 'The Liberator'

The Liberator Series is a ferocious new collaboration between Luke Richardson and Amazon Bestseller, Steven Moore.

If you like Clive Cussler, Nick Thacker, Ernest Dempsey and Rusesel Blake, then you'll love this explosive new series!

www.lukerichardsonauthor.com/theliberator

THANK YOU

Thank you for reading my first novel. The completion of this book has been the dream of many years.

The story of the lamb and the restaurant has been going around in my mind for a long time, so long that I can't remember how I first came across it. But it wasn't until I visited Kathmandu that I put the two together, along with our nervous investigator, Leo.

As may come across in my writing, travelling, exploring and seeing the world is so important to me, as is coming home to my family and friends.

Although the words here are my own, the characters, experiences and some of the events described are wholly inspired by the people I've travelled beside.

If we ever shared noodles from a street-food vendor, visited a temple together, played cards on a creaking overnight train, or had a beer in a back-street restaurant, you are forever in this book, and for that, I thank you too!

It is the intention of my writing to show that although the world is big and the unknown can be unsettling, there is so much good in it. Although the men in the restaurant and people traffickers are bad, evil people, I think they are vastly outnumbered by the honesty, purity and kindness of the other characters. You don't have to look far to see this in the real world. I know that whenever I travel, it's the kindness of the people that I remember, almost more than the place itself.

Whether you're an experienced traveller, or you prefer your home turf, I hope this story has taken you somewhere new and exciting — even if you've been to Kathmandu and found the backstreet restaurant.

Again, thank you for coming on the adventure with me. I hope to see you again.

Luke
(March 2019)

PS. A little warning, next time someone talks to you in the airport, be careful what you say, as you may end up in their book.

BOOK REVIEWS

If you've enjoyed this book I would appreciate a review.

Reviews are essential for three reasons. Firstly, they encourage people to take a chance on an author they've never heard of. Secondly, bookselling websites use them to decide what books to recommend through their search engine. And third, I love to hear what you think!

Having good reviews really can make a massive difference to new authors like me.

It'll take you no longer than two minutes, and will mean the world to me.

www.lukerichardsonauthor.com/reviews

Thank you.

Printed in Great Britain
by Amazon